SUBVERSIVES

For Beverley!
Enjoy!
Ellee Shannon

ISBN: 978-1-7288227-7-8

AUTHOR'S ACKNOWLEDGMENTS

Colleagues and former students have been indispensable to my preparation for this project. Thank you to teacher friends Melissa Leighton Mueller and Dave McGregor, for updating me on the use of tech in the classroom and the protocol for student safety drills. And to Chuck Melki for his patience with this student, who came into his gun range knowing not one thing about firearms.

And to Dave Hedges, who knows how to plan a party. And to Gene O'Kelly, who has saved more lives than he will ever know.

Thank you to my generous friend Bob Fleury for insisting that I had a story to tell, for the cover design and for his expertise in publishing.

And most of all to the community of subversives, the observant, caring adults who keep our young people safe.

"Stop right there."

———————————————————

.

SUBVERSIVES

BY

ELLIE SHARROW

SUBVERSIVES

Beginning of the end

"Hey there! You stopping by Duffy's today?"

Mike Bagley taught history down the hall. His head popped through the door, the din of exodus in the hallway behind him.

It was Friday. Payday. Of course she was stopping by Duffy's. Happy hour, after all.

"Sure. I'll be out of here shortly. Just need to load up my weekend reading."

She slid the MacBook into her tote bag, gathered her coat from the classroom closet and fished out her keys. A flick of the light switch and she was out the door. A cold beer with fellow teachers was a relaxing way to unwind from the work week. The faculty lot emptied a bit quicker on paydays.

Friday was also the day the creative writing class submitted their weekly journals. She had considered switching turn-in day to Thursday, certain that she could get them all read by the next day. That way some of the kids could use the weekend to catch up on their writing if they wanted to. Plus it would let her enjoy her own weekends rather than postponing journal reading until Sunday evening. Monday she would announce the change to the class.

At first, the kids thought that creative writing might be a blow-off class. Creative, right? Couldn't really put a grade on creativity, right? They had learned quickly, however, that there were plenty of other things that could be graded, and they would have to work. The class attracted the "right" students now. Those who really enjoyed flexing their mental muscles.

She pushed through the door to the neighborhood watering hole. Looks like the crowd with last hour prep managed to get to the bar ahead of her, having moved a bunch of tables into a long row to accommodate the crowd. There would be gossip, shop talk, flirting and laughter for a couple hours before the gang would break up and go home to family dinners.

Janet didn't rush home. Her cat would be glad to see her and demand his dinner, but no husband or family needed her to cook for them. She was 30 and single, subletting a condo in a complex just outside of town. It was an easy commute and a pleasant neighborhood. She was glad to have found a teaching position here. She knew college friends who had taken jobs in larger districts who weren't as lucky.

She pulled into the carport, locked the Honda, and went in to feed Toby.

Her phone rang.

"Hi, Charley." She listened.

"You know, that is a great idea, but could I get a raincheck? I could not possibly go out again tonight." Good lord, was she turning into her grandma?

"Okay. Talk tomorrow. Bye."

She kicked off her shoes and reached under her shirt to unhook her bra. Time for sweats and Netflix.

A trip through the kitchen. Nuked the leftover pizza. Grabbed her phone and her laptop and plopped down onto the couch.

Let's see what the kiddos gave me this time. The assignment was a page a day of journaling, with wide latitude on content.

The bell rang for the last class period of the day to begin. Twenty-five juniors and seniors looked at her curiously, their laptops open in front of them. It was the first day of the second semester. Afternoon winter sun lit up the room, reflected by the snow outside. She introduced herself and had them each introduce themselves to her and the rest of the class. This was a silly thing to do, but nobody minded. Most of them had known each other their whole lives. Most of them had already taken a Language Arts class from Janet Miller. She was known to expect a lot, but she also had a sense of humor, which made it bearable.

"You are here to write, and you should expect to write in class every day. Fridays are author days. You may choose what to share with the class on author days. And the journal is actually a significant part of your grade," she explained.

"Plan to write a page a day. Each day may be a separate piece of writing, or you may combine them. They may be about anything you want to write. I promise I will never read your journals out loud in the lounge and laugh. I will respect your privacy. Plan to submit a folder of five pages every Friday. I will give you feedback, but not a grade. The purpose is to improve your writing over time. I will log the number of pages you submit. Yes, John?"

The young man leaned back, easy in his chair, long legs sprawling.

"What if we write things you don't like? You know, politics or hunting or something."

"Well, We might have some interesting things to talk about then. We don't expect to agree about everything. Part of this will be finding your own voice. If you're really asking about "language" - with an exaggerated eye roll - demonstrate your good judgment. You know what is appropriate and what is not. The teenagers laughed out loud at the eye-roll. She was famous for her number one rule about the juvenile expression of disrespect. "Now. Who has a favorite author?"

The period passed quickly as they discovered that they each had a favorite author, even if some of them were sports columnists not novelists. An argument about the legitimacy of graphic novels as literature rounded out the hour.

At the end of the first week, Jan opened John's journal folder.

There's been another shooting at some mall out west. Every time these happen, the libtards go batshit crazy. They are blind to what is happening in this country. When it all goes down, they are going to be pounding on our door

begging for protection. We are going
to need our guns then, and they
will finally admit that they were
wrong and we were right all along.

Oh my goodness, she thought. I had no idea he was a gun nut. This must be what he meant that first day when he asked about writing something I might not like. Libtard! That's just about my least favorite word. Well, he won't rattle me! We'll see how this pans out.

The Author's Chair was a funky throwback. Made of wood, it had once been a teacher's chair and sat behind a matching wooden desk. She had picked it out of a heap of old furniture headed for the dump, crammed it into the Honda, and took it home for updating. It was reborn as a gaudy throne painted in brightly colored enamels. Most of the week it sat in a corner, unused. On Fridays it was pulled out front and center. It worked like a talking stick or the conch in Lord of the Flies. Whoever wanted to read first would claim their spot in the chair before the bell rang. The rest of the group listened quietly to the sharing of scenes and poems and reflections on events. Then came comments. On the first Author Day those comments were all very pleasant.

"Oh, I really like that."

"That was so good."

Ms. Miller's comments were encouraging as well, but more specific. She pointed out interesting word choices or particularly vivid descriptions. It did not take long for the students to pick up on the difference, and their own contributions became more precise.

The second Author's Day presented a quick paced narration about a princess fleeing a dragon, hopping over walls and dodging impediments. The writer was really into the cadence and after a few minutes John burst out laughing. What's funny? Is he being rude? The reader didn't seem to mind, and then the others caught onto the joke. It was the plot line of a vintage video game. Everybody laughed and clapped when it was over.

This was getting to be fun.

Jan had noticed that a couple of the students seemed reluctant to participate. Shy, probably. She made a point of finding suitable passages in their journals for sharing aloud. Daric's journal, so far, had been filled with rap lyrics. She really didn't know if they were original or simply things that he liked. She asked, in the margin, in purple ink. He ignored the inquiry. Okay then. A tough nut. Daric was one of the few Black students in the school. The diversity data indicated enrollment was 89% Caucasian, 6.2% Hispanic, 4.6% African American, the rest Other. The Others were Pacific Islanders and siblings. The eldest and most self assured occasionally substituted Other for his actual surname on school documents. He liked to mess with The Man, and The Man was good natured about it. The students were aware of administrative obsession with data. The minorities were aware of the importance of their academic success to the numbers. It seemed to Daric that some of his teachers fawned over every little achievement. He was very bright, endlessly bored, and contemptuous of anyone's lowered expectations. The raps in his journal were defiant. Messing with the pretty blonde. Funny. One of these days he would surprise her. Surprise everyone. He had been journaling for over a year and not for any class. One of these Fridays.

The following week's lesson had been creating dialogue. She had suggested eavesdropping on casual conversation and trying to catch its tone. They left class that day eager to spy on their unsuspecting friends. By the next morning, the talk in the hall was about a near fight between locker neighbors when one noticed the other recording his bragging. And Linda stopped by Ms. Miller's room between classes, in near tears.

"Last night my mom got really mad at me because I was just doing my assignment," she said. "She was so mean about it."

So much for realism. She had forgotten about fictionalizing life to protect the innocent.

So that was what they talked about in Creative Writing class that day.

"Let's imagine a scene that takes place in a small bakery. Who might be there? The lady behind the counter."

"That's Connie!"

"Right, but let's change her name for this. That way you can make her different, like not Connie.

"Who else? A customer buying bread? Another customer on his laptop, at a table? What might these people look like? How might they interact? As neighbors? Or strangers? Have them talk. Now write it. I'm going to stop you in a few minutes."

They turned to their keyboards and the room filled with soft clicking. After fifteen minutes, she interrupted them.

"Who's got something to share?"

"But it's not even Author's Day?" Of course that was

Linda.

"I can count it if you like."

Daric lifted his hand.

She nodded at him. He read.

A bell jingled as a pair of customers entered. Young guys with backpacks. Quick scan of the small shop. "Yo." Apparently to the only other dude there, sitting at a small table with a coffee. He nodded.

A smiling white lady in a floury apron emerged from the kitchen in the back. "Well, hello fellas! Can I get you something?"

"Yeah, a couple carrot muffins. Extra fiber."

She opened the glass case, selected two carrot muffins. "You want them to go, or you going to eat them here?"

"Better stick 'em in a bag. Thanks." He pulled a five from his pocket. She turned to the old fashioned cash register to make the change. Put the muffins into a white bakery bag and handed them over the counter. She lingered. It was obvious. The second guy had been watching the dude with the coffee.

"Wha'choo lookin' at?"

"Not much." The dude pulled

out his phone and switched on the recorder. He set the phone on the table next to the coffee mug.

"Let's get outta here, asshole."

"Right."

"Asshole."

They left with a soft jingling of a bell.

The audience erupted with questions.

"What was that?"

"I thought something had to happen."

"Didn't you see what happened?"

"He said 'asshole'. That's bad language. Are you going to kick him out?" Linda again.

"Wait. Were the guys black? They were, weren't they?"

"That was Connie. I know that was Connie. She is just like that."

Daric almost smiled.

"So the bakery lady was white. What about the guys? You didn't say. Why didn't you say?"

Ms. Miller intervened. "Does it matter? How did they seem to you? What could you guess about the young men? Do you think they were friends? Did they know each other?"

"I think they did, but they were not friends."

Daric smiled. They were getting it.

The bell rang.

Later that afternoon Jan pulled the Honda into a spot in front of the bakery. Last hour reminded her how good Connie's bagels were. She pushed the door open to a light jingle. Summoned, Connie emerged from the kitchen. Jan smiled to see her apron. Flowery and floury.

"Hi, Connie. Could you get me a couple fresh bagels? To go. Thanks."

She spotted him at the corner table. Daric had his laptop out. Probably Instagram, but she hoped he was writing. She wandered near his table.

"That was a nice piece of writing today. I'm glad you decided to share it."

"Thanks, ma'am. I like to write."

"Well, you set the bar for yourself today. They are going to want more, you know."

"Yes, I figured that might happen."

"Just between us, about the two other guys. Who were they? Do you know?"

"Of course I know." He looked back at his screen. The teacher had been dismissed.

"Ok then. See you tomorrow."

She didn't wait to get home to toast her bagel. She pulled it out of the bag and nibbled as she drove home. She was looking forward to journal day. Somehow she figured it would not be rap lyrics this time.

The bakery had been a popular spot in town since before the beginning of wifi. The interior had been preserved rather than remodeled. Tin ceiling, wooden floor, museum quality glass fronted bakery cases. The kitchen had been updated in a recent century. Adjacent to a coffee shop, senior citizens gathered in the mornings for a cuppa and company. The after lunch visitors were often young parents with toddlers stopping by for a cookie. Connie had worked there for years and knew almost everyone by name. After school the high school kids came in, those that did not have team practice. The coffee shop stayed open evenings, but the adjacent bakery closed at 3 so they hustled downtown as soon as school got out. The tables filled with laptops while the multi-taskers juggled research, homework, and social media. Some bought coffee drinks, some didn't. All were welcome unless they got too rowdy or tried to bring in snacks from outside. That was where Connie drew the line. The last rowdy group to be kicked out were the Vietnam vets. Connie acted as bouncer. The after dinner crowd tended to be the college kids who often met up and then wandered down the block to Duffy's.

Everyone in the writing class recognized the setting of Daric's story. John knew it. He stopped by his locker. Pulled on a camo jacket and an old wool knit cap. Grabbed his backpack and headed out. The crowd parted for him, not that he noticed. He spoke to no one. The hat had belonged to his Dad from his days in the Marines. He never talked about those times, but he kept the hat. John had worn his dad's hat and jacket every cold day since.

The walk to the bakery took 15 minutes.

On this afternoon John stopped in and headed for a quiet corner table. He beat the crowd, apparently. He pulled his laptop from his backpack and opened it. He leaned against the wall and watched the front door.

The bell jingled. Three girls headed into the coffee shop, laughing, eyes scanning for friends. Linda. Crap. She separated from the others and settled alone at a table. Out came the laptop. She bent over the keyboard, apparently focused on some task. John watched her pause and look around the shop. She returned to her work. Crap. She's writing about this place, John thought. He quickly

11

packed up and slipped out the alley door.

Next Authors Day brought three bakery scenes. John did not read that day, but he felt relieved anyway.

John Kerr and his mother Marian lived outside of town where small houses on big lots with pole barns out back were the norm.

His father Marcus survived a Marine deployment, and then died when John was 16 after a bad equipment accident. Before he died in the emergency room, he had asked his son to take care of his mom, and John promised that he would. Now that promise was weighing on John's mind as high school graduation approached. He hadn't applied to college like the other seniors had done, convinced that his dad would see that as the breaking of a solemn promise. At the same time, he didn't see himself staying here forever, and his mother, unaware of the deathbed promise, wanted to see her only child thrive and be happy. John was torn.

He was his dad's boy, trailing him as a toddler, then going with him to the gun range when he was old enough to learn to shoot. They enjoyed hunting deer and the annual deer camp was a favorite family tradition. A week in the north woods with his father, uncles and couple cousins. A week of guys being guys. The youngsters and their dads doing their own cooking, drinking beer, and not shaving. Pissing in the woods. Out at dawn and bucks on the pole by the end of the week.

Marian had stayed home with her little son for the first few years. She loved taking care of her fellas. She was a good cook, and had actually prepared the meals that went off to deer camp with them. She had never quite trusted the fellas to keep themselves from starving. When

John started school, she brought in extra money by baking pies for a popular truck stop off the interstate. The manager there gave her a standing order for five pies every day. After her husband's death, she secured full time employment there, where she contentedly took care of the fellas who were enroute across the Midwest and hungry for a good meal.

In high school, John had few friends because he mostly kept to himself. He was not an athlete, despite encouragement by various coaches. He just wasn't interested. He attended a couple football games each fall, and hoops if the team made it to Districts. Otherwise he chose to spend his time shooting bottles out behind the pole barn. Army recruiters visited the school, and he stopped by their table at lunch time one day. After the most recent deer camp he had decided against military service. His uncles pointed out the fruitlessness of war in the mideast that had been dragging on for decades. No, that wasn't going to be his life. The recruiters had tried their best by appealing to his interests, and since his main interest was shooting things, they figured he was their guy. He said no thanks, as firmly as he could, but things still came in the mail for him from the US Army. The army. As if.

John had signed up for creative writing because he needed one more credit in English and was loathe to give speeches. Don't even get him started on Drama. Writing he figured he could do.

"So, looks like the bakery was a good suggestion," Ms Miller said in class the next day. "It cannot possibly be the only place you know where you can create a fictional scene. Let's play a little game today. Take this slip of paper and write a real place somewhere around town. We're going to put them into this bowl."

"Now everyone pull out a slip. We'll do a little quick write, no more than 200 words, just to rev up your brain."

The bowl was passed. "Oh, no. Can't do that one." That slip was returned to the bowl and switched for another.

Jan wandered the room while the kids tapped away. Cemetery. Riverbank. Bandshell. Police department. Gun shop. Cemetery again, Farmers Market. Picnic pavilion. Bowling alley. Hmm, she thought, this could work.

John continued to lean back in his chair, eyes half closed. Defiance? Sloth? She chose to ignore whatever he was doing, for now.

"Who's got something interesting? Anyone?"

The rest of the period passed quickly with reads. Most were descriptive using first person point of view. No one injected another character or any dialogue. The various sites were described clearly, and, she noticed, most seemed to be taking place on sunny afternoons after school. She called their attention to that and suggested varying either the time of day or the weather. Looked like several of them might take her up on that.

On his 18th birthday Marian had presented her son with a safe deposit box key. The box had not been opened since her husband's death although she made sure the rental was current. She took a copy of her husband's death certificate along when she and her grown son went to the bank. The business added John's name to the box and removed the late Marcus. Then she let John take the heavy box into a service room.

He had no idea that his father had been a collector of handguns. All he had ever used were the deer rifles. He never talked about home security, but John knew there was a 12 gauge in the corner of his parents' closet. The box in front of him contained an assortment of handguns. He removed them one by one, photographing them one at a time with his phone. He could not identify them by sight, but the photos would help with that.

John skipped the bakery that day and instead headed the other way to check out the gun shop. He would have something interesting to read on Friday.

Daric knew all the places suggested in the day's exercise. Unlike most of the students, he had not lived here his whole life, but the town just wasn't that big. An hour's walk around downtown was all it took to see it all. His family had moved from Baltimore last summer to spend his senior year at a new school. He was putting in the time until he could graduate and move back east. While John headed into the gun shop, Daric wandered toward the river. The sky was the same dirty white as the dirty ice piles edging the park. Winter had been heavy. A sudden warming had melted the snow and the river was running high, over its banks in spots. He pulled his phone out and flicked on the camera for shots of the rushing gray water and the trunk of a large dead tree pulled along like it was a canoe. Ducks perched on the log. She wants the riverbank? She'll get the riverbank.

The Richardson family had moved from Baltimore last summer, when his father, a biological engineer, had been transferred to oversee a new project in the middle of flyover country. Daric knew it was a good move for his dad's career and he had avoided whining about the move. He had left that to his sister who whined enough for the whole family. She was in love, you see, and certain that she would forever be denied that bliss if she was dragged away. Find a good looking brother who wasn't her brother? Not even a chance. Daric was closer to graduation and the freedom to return to civilization. He never mentioned his early acceptance into NYU to anyone at his new school. No need to know, he figured. Meanwhile he had discovered the small town bakery was a convenient place to work.

A row of pickups parked in front of Short's Shots. No sweet little bell announced arrivals. Inside, a thick rack of shirts and jackets crowded the door. Narrow aisles separated packed displays of firearm paraphernalia: sights and scopes and holsters and targets and noise reduction ear plugs, plus recreational drones and other toys, piled with no evident organization. The middle contrasted with the tidy and organized glass cases that lined three sides of the small, crowded shop. Shiny cases were filled with neat rows of handguns down the right side, long guns down the left side, and boxes of ammo across the back. A motley display of assault firearms ranged high on the walls, out of easy reach.

A burly guy wearing tattoo sleeves under a patriotic tee shirt stood behind the rear counter. "Can I help you find anything?"

"Actually I have a few photos I'd like you to look at."

John pulled the phone from his pocket and opened the photos. One flipped through the photos while the other made notes.

A revolver, 38 Special

Four semi-automatics: a .38 Winchester, a .38 Smith

& Wesson, a .45 Colt, and a 9mm Glock.

"You interested in selling any of these?" the shop guy asked. "They all look like new. Not used much, I bet."

"I'll let you know. Not sure yet. They were my dad's. But while I am here, I would like to look at that AR15 you got up there."

The Teachers Meeting

After the students had left for the day, the faculty made their way to the library for the monthly teachers meeting. Food services provided a tray of fresh cookies and coffee, the scent of which lured lingerers into the room. They were surprised to see state troopers and a canine unit standing with the principal at the front. Jan scanned the room for friends and joined them at a table in the middle.

"That's a good looking German Shepherd that cop's got."

"That's a good looking trooper that dog's got."

"No kidding. I wonder if we will get a demo of dog training today."

The principal took a few steps forward. "Okay, everyone, let's get started here. I know you don't want to be here any longer than necessary, but your contracts say I get to keep you a little later today."

He stood next to the dreaded flip chart.

The room quieted.

"As we all know, the news reminds us every week that schools can be dangerous places. Some time in the next two weeks we will be holding a lockdown drill in the building. We all need to be prepared so that the students in our charge will respond properly to our directions.

This drill will be a bit different than ones we've run in the past. One or more troopers will be firing blanks in the hallways so that students may become familiar with the sound of gunshots. This will be a very realistic drill.

"Now I want to introduce Trooper Jackson from the Gaylord post with his canine unit, Charge. The state officer stepped forward, Charge close to his left knee.

"You probably have seen drug dogs and bomb-sniffing dogs. Charge here has a different super power. Charge detects firearms. It doesn't matter what kind of firearm, loaded or unloaded, he can locate it. Charge and I will respond to a call when a firearm has been reported inside a school. He can check all the lockers in a building of this size much faster than staff could do it, and without necessarily evacuating the building. And he can work a crowd to find a concealed carry just as easily."

The teachers looked around at each other, laughing nervously.

"Before you all arrived here this afternoon, I asked Rob, your gym teacher here, to hide an unloaded firearm in this library.

"Charge, find it."

The sleek beast set off on a clockwise perimeter of the large library. He stopped in front of the current periodicals rack and sat, staring down at the display. Rob laughed. "He found it!"

Then Charge turned quickly and trotted between the tables toward the rear where the science department usually sat together. He stopped in front of Charley Keyes, the AP Chem teacher, and sat.

"Uh-oh. Charley's busted." From the math contingent. Laughter was scattered and uncomfortable.

After the meeting Charley would produce his CPL and discuss the matter with building administration. Schools were gun free zones, and firearms were not covered in the teacher contract. In the meantime the group reviewed procedures for the coming drill. When it was time to leave, no one was in the mood for Duffy's. Janet Miller felt exhausted and near tears.

The drill came the next day.

"Good afternoon, everyone. It is time to initiate the procedures for a lockdown drill. We will let you know when the drill has been concluded."

Thank god, Janet Miller thought. A drill during her planning period meant she did not have to corral a class into hiding. She could just as well stay in the teachers workroom and get things done.

The building grew quiet except for some heavy bootsteps passing the door and the soft skittering of a dog's nails on the terrazzo flooring. Charge is here, she thought, opening the door and peeking down the hall. She was really interested in observing the dog at work. He trotted near the row of lockers, untempted by any of them. Around the corner went the canine unit and his hot handler. She left the workroom and followed them.

The drills had become routine in all districts since the growing concern about school safety. She knew that most of the kids would be huddled on the floor in a corner of the classroom, texting their friends. The drill provided a chance for everyone to catch up on their social media.

Bam! Bam!

The shots sounded nothing like in the movies.

Jan ducked into the girls room at the unexpected gunshots. The teachers had been cautioned to expect them; the students were unprepared. She found half a dozen teenagers cowering there. There were tears. She offered hugs and reassurance she did not feel. They agreed to stay right where they were.

Minutes passed.

Heavy footsteps, running.

Then, from the speakers, "This is the all clear. The drill is completed. Good job, everybody. Thank you for your cooperation."

Whose voice was that? None of the females wanted to leave the bathroom. When the bell sounded to signal the end of the period, the building returned to life. Normal crowd-of-teenagers sounds from the hall. The girls washed the tears from their faces, refreshed their mascara, and rejoined the throng outside the door. Janet headed back to her room for the last hour, creative writing. She recognized a teachable moment tossed into her lap: recreating the sensations of fear. This is one she wanted to write for herself.

The class assembled more quickly than usual. She guessed no one wanted to be out in that hall a second longer than necessary.

"Did you hear those shots?"

"What was that all about?"

"They cannot be shooting guns off inside the school

like that."

The bell rang and no one paid any attention to it.

Jan had recovered her composure enough to step into teacher mode. "Okay, everyone. I don't know about you, but I thought that was pretty darn terrifying."

The group exchanged looks. Duh, clearly.

"In fact, before I forget how I felt, I want to write it down. Right now. How did it feel to be scared to death?"

"You want us to write right now?"

"I can't do it," Linda gasped. "That was just too awful."

"Yes. It was awful. But we are okay now. It is over. And I want you to recreate the sensation of your fear."

They understood what she was doing. They opened their laptops. A few minutes later they were clamoring to read. Eager to see who was the most scared? Maybe. This could be a competitive bunch.

When the final bell ended their unusual day, the quick writing exercise had vented most of the emotion. Dismissal felt pretty normal.

Not everyone had read their quick writes. Jan opened the Creative Writing folder in Classroom to check what the other students had written. She found John's first.

He had ignored the assignment about the feeling of fear. Instead he related his visit to Short Shots and his personal arsenal and the assault rifle he liked the feel of, and that he was thinking about buying.

She was horrified to realize the feelings of fear had returned.

Rescue Me

Linda Johnson was not exactly plain, and in fact, in the next couple of years she would blossom into a not unattractive young woman. So a late bloomer, with all the insecurities that come with that for a teenage girl. She had a best friend who would double cross her in a heartbeat. She lived with two parents who didn't seem to like each other very much and two sisters with whom she shared a bathroom. Their house was a noisy place. Mom was a yeller. The tv was on all day long at high volume. Dad drove truck and away from home overnight once a week, at least. While she knew her own life provided no useable inspiration, Linda fancied herself a poet which is why she had signed up for the creative writing class.

While she felt everything intensely, the afternoon of the lockdown drill provided more than the usual drama. After school she headed toward the business district and the bakery. Today warranted a coffee and a cookie. She deserved it after all that. As soon as she entered she spotted Daric at his favorite table. That one was really attractive, but there was no way he would ever even want to talk to her. She could almost feel the eye-roll every time she opened her mouth in class. She took her coffee and cookie to a corner where she could watch Daric without being obvious. He was working on his laptop. Maybe she could do the same. Maybe a poem about a princess being rescued from a lunatic by a handsome Black hero.

There was no way he could have approached her table without her knowing. Still.

"Hey, Linda. You doin' okay? That was wild, wasn't it."

"Oh. Daric. That was the worst thing ever." Then she burst into tears. It quickly became an ugly cry. Streaming mascara, snot bubbles and all.

His father would have had a clean handkerchief for this unexpected event. A handful of paper napkins would do in a pinch. He grabbed them from the next table and handed them to the messy white girl.

"Please don't you worry about it. Now we know how gunshots sound. If it ever happens for real, we will know what is going on. That is the point of these drills. They sure are a pain in the ass."

"Oh, I guess you're right about that. I hope I never hear a gunshot again." She mopped up the sniffles as best she could. "Thanks, Daric, you really are a nice guy. Nicer than I ever thought."

It was just some paper napkins, he thought, but tried to accept the odd compliment. He worried about her. She was really kind of a mess. "Are you going home soon?"

"I probably should." Big sigh.

"How about if I walk part way with you."

"Oh. All right." And those feelings of fear returned. Or maybe it was something else. Something for a poem.

Happy Hour

The following payday saw the usual crew arriving at Duffy's for happy hour. Six teachers were already there when Jan joined them. She tossed her coat over the back of her chair and collapsed into it.

"Somebody get me a Stella!" Her friends laughed. They all shared the relief of a completed week. The waitress stopped by with a loaded tray.

"Does anybody know if we are finished with drills for the year?" Charley asked.

"I don't mind another drill if that gorgeous guy with the dog comes back," said Fran, the faculty flirt from business ed.

"If you want to meet him off the clock," someone else suggested, "just head out to the interstate and drive real fast."

"I don't think the canine patrols go out after speeders. He's probably going around to schools full time scaring the hell out of everybody."

"We really need to talk about something else," said Jan. "Just about anything else will do. How about our basketball brackets? Who's got 'em?"

Conversation turned to March Madness. Jan didn't really care about college basketball. She found the voices of her colleagues comforting as they laughed and bantered about favorite teams.

Charley, the chem teacher, joined them and sat next to Jan.

She turned to him. "Can I ask you something about that faculty meeting?"

"About was I packing heat? Yeah, I always carry. It's not something I wanted everybody to know about because I figured it might make some people nervous. I told Ernie about it after the demo was over. I think he was embarrassed because of the dog, you know, but I think he was kind of relieved, too. He didn't say I should stop. Do you still like me?"

Jan chuckled. "Oh, Charley, I think I am relieved too. Maybe I need to think about it, but yes, I still like you. I know we need to be ready for anything, but kids should not have to think about getting shot in school."

"Yo, Charley, my man! Let me buy you a beer. That dog busting you for carrying was the funniest part of the whole teachers meeting."

Charley stood up and took an exaggerated bow while his colleagues hooted and cheered.

"Well, I do what I can," he admitted with false modesty. "How long do you think it will take for the kids to find out? As if that kind of news would stay secret.

The Free Day

Jan was surprised early Monday morning to get a text announcing school was closed on Monday due to a threat. She showered quickly, pulled on jeans and a sweater, and raced to the high school. A dozen cars were parked in the teacher lot and three state police cars were positioned strategically. No students. They were smart and no doubt got the notice and rolled over and went back to sleep.

Principal Ernie White stood talking with Charge's handler. Looked like they were about to tour the building.

"Please, Ernie. What's happened? The call said you had a threat?"

"Yes, Jan, we did. Apparently something was online. A student found it and called the hotline. I did not actually see the threat myself, but the police here take any threat very seriously so we called school to give them time to check things out."

"So there might not have been a threat at all, really?"

Charley joined the group outside the school. Apparently Charge recognized him. He wagged his tail. Trooper Jackson opened the door. "Charge, find it." Charge promptly sat in front of Charley. Jan swallowed a laugh.

"Come in, Charge. Find it." And so the building search began. It took only a few minutes for the two teachers to become bored with this endeavor. They climbed into the Honda and headed to the bakery for some fresh coffee. It was a busy place. Teenagers had joined the usual senior citizens. Connie was smiling and greeted everyone by name. Closing the school was good for business.

A dozen phones pinged simultaneously with the All Clear text. Classes would resume the next day. The crowd in the bakery cheered. An unexpected day off could be enjoyed by all, but no one wanted to see actual destruction or injury at the school. Charley and Jan drove back to the school. One state police unit remained, the engine running.

In the office a serious meeting was underway. What should be done about a student making a false threat to the hot line, but maintain the see something-say something position? Had the student actually seen something online that he perceived to be a threat? Could he find it again so they could evaluate its merit? Clearly they needed to speak to that student. Whoever he was. There was no doubt that it was a male.

The news that evening reported multiple threats at schools across the state. Police took all of them seriously, the reporter said.

Retiree

Connie had had to ask Bill Knott and a couple cronies to leave the bakery that one time when their conversation was too loud and profane to suit her. He had opinions about the state of the nation and society's decline since the 1970's when young people started smoking all that pot and women left their homes for careers when that was completely unnecessary. He had never married and had no children of his own, but after the Marines he visited a buddy's classroom, loved the energy and just knew that teaching was what he wanted to do next.

"Show your work!" he bellowed in algebra class.

Once a Marine, always a Marine. His height, fitness and volume terrified many of the sixth graders he taught. So they showed their work.

His reputation was as a strict disciplinarian with a paddle sitting on the chalk ledge. He rarely used it. Never, actually.

But that was all years ago. Now he was long retired, a recognized character around town, holding court at the breakfast-only place, ranting about politics and the state of the world from a regular table with a bunch of the other old men.

"What's with all the kids downtown today? Don't they have school?"

"Heard they closed today. Something about a threat to shoot the place up."

"What?" Bill acted shocked. "How did that happen? I tell ya, they just don't have the discipline any more. But shoot the place up? Parents these days are just not up to the job. But you know the grandparents were all smoking the pot back in the day."

"Naw, Bill. Pot had nothing to do with it," said Chuck. "Those silly hippies were too stoned to find their way out of the basement. Useless! But you gotta admit there's an awful lot of guns floating around out there. Some crazy kid can get their old man's gun and just march into school waving it around. It's all over the news."

"Yeah, that's true." Bill shook his head in disgust. "They don't know what they're doing. When I got out of the Marines, I was done with that. Saw enough In 'Nam to last ten lifetimes. Kids today play too many video games. That's what's behind it, you know. Listen to Fox. They say it all the time. The crazy libs want to take the guns away, but they should be taking those violent games away. Warp young minds, they do! The kids are crazy and their parents let them get that way."

And Bill Knott was not the only one who thought that way.

He pulled on his camo jacket and watch cap, paid his bill, and left with a wave of his hand.

Down the block John was tapping away at his laptop when the little bell jingled and he became aware of a presence. A tall man loomed over him.

"Excuse me," the tall man said, "I was looking at your hat."

John laughed, surprised. They wore matching black wool watch caps. Hey! How about that?

"Hello, Mr. Knott!" It was Connie. "I have some fresh seeded rye here, that kind you like. Want me to slice a loaf for you?"

"Yeah, sure, Connie. Thanks."

He continued to John. "I don't think I've ever seen a young fella like you wearing the watch cap. You're a little young for the Marines, amiright?"

The electric slicer made a loud racket.

"Yes, sir. It was my dad's. He was in the Marines, in Afghanistan. But he's dead now."

"Sorry, son. Marines stick together. They teach us that."

The old man paid for his bread and nodded to the young man as he left the shop.

"Jan, you're close to the kids. They tell you stuff. Have you heard anything about this threat business?" Principal Ernie White was on his way out of the meeting that had not yielded any clues. He hoped to get the phone number that had called the hotline. It might not lead to anything, but then again, it might.

Jan took her time. "Everybody seemed shocked and scared during the drill last week. I didn't see anybody looking eager to give it a go. I'll keep my ears open tomorrow. Somebody may start bragging and that will spread."

Certainly John was not the only guy with guns at home. And you don't even need a gun to just call that hotline. Hell, it could be anybody.

"The kids got a free day yesterday. We may hear a whole lot of bragging going on, claiming it. I'll let you know if I hear anything."

"Trooper Jackson said he'd nose around that gun shop and see if they've had interest from teenagers lately."

Jan decided she would share that idea with Charley. He'd know how likely the owner of Short Shots would rat out a customer. She sure would not rat out a student over a journal entry. Not that it was the confessional, but she had promised to respect their privacy, and she took that promise seriously. Unless the entry explicitly threatened to hurt somebody. Then all bets were off.

"See you tomorrow, Jan. We'll try it again."

She texted Charley from the Honda.

Pizza and beer?
Sounds great.
Meet you at Duffy's?
Half hour

Quick stop at home for a hairbrush and a little makeup. She had left in a rush this morning. Not that this was a date, but still. No need to scare the guy.

She met Charley on the sidewalk and they walked in together. The place was quieter today. No crowd of celebrating teachers. They took a small table and gave their order to the waitress. An older man sat at the next table. She had seen him around town a few times and knew him by reputation, but he had retired while she was still in high school. She nodded to him and smiled. Maybe someday she would be a legend, like him.

32

She glanced around the dim bar. Nobody else within earshot.

"Charley, Ernie told me that trooper was going down to the gun shop looking for leads. What do you think about that? Do you know who owns that place?"

"I haven't been in there myself," he said, "but I suspect the owner would be suspicious of a cop snooping around. Unless one came in with a subpoena, he would not volunteer information about a customer. That word would get around pretty quick."

"Is the gun business really that sketchy?"

"I wouldn't call it sketchy. I'd say paranoid. A third of the people in this state own guns, and the rest hates them."

"How long have you owned a gun?"

"I grew up around guns. My family hunted, and the kids all learned gun safety before we learned to drive. I enjoy going out to the range because target shooting is fun, and I'm friends with the guys there. Some people golf. I shoot."

"But why did you decide to carry a gun at school?"

Charley looked past Jan at the old guy eavesdropping from the next table.

"I have been in the habit of wearing a pistol for years, not just at school. I figure if I see somebody in trouble, being hurt, I could step in and help. Haven't had to, thank god."

Their pizza arrived ending serious conversation.

At the next table, Mr. Knott nodded. He knew Charley from the range, and by tacit agreement, they kept it there.

Copycat

According to the news, many schools around the state had experienced copycat threats of violence in recent days. People who had not been inside a school in decades insisted it was just crazy kids getting time off. Teachers debated the copycats over lunch. The racket in the hallways was just a bit louder than usual, Jan thought, the laughing a bit more, an effort to hide the truth that the kids were on edge.

Principal White invited his head of security to join him in the office, door closed. The office staff knew something was going on in there and headed off any interruptions. At his desk, White cued up the hotline. The two men leaned forward, listening.

"Um. Hello. I'm not sure how this thing is supposed to work, but I found something today that you probably need to know about. It's a note that was on the bus going home. It says, 'Shooting up everybody I hate all those faggots.' So that's it. Bye."

Nick shrugged.

"Not much to go on, really," said White.

"On the afternoon bus, eh? Get a list of all the riders. Probably not one of the older guys. They usually ditch the cheesebox as soon as they can drive."

Mr. White called the bus barn office. The list would be coming ASAP.

"Thanks, Nick. Let me know if you hear anything."

Nick left the office just as the bell rang. Showtime! The teachers did their thing in the classrooms. Nick did his everywhere else, in the halls, at their lockers, in the parking lot.

Nick O'Reilly had worked security in this building for decades. At one point early in his career he had been voted Most Trusted Adult in the Building. It was an informal poll conducted by that year's yearbook staff, but no one ever contested the results. He was the favorite uncle and keeper of secrets. More counseling happened in doorways than ever did in the offices of the professionals. He was a good man and highly respected. And he knew the kid whose voice he had just heard on that recording. He would run into him in the usual place today.

That place was the door at the south end of the building, outside the cafeteria.

"Hey, Carl, how you doin' today? Have you heard back from State yet?"

That was not the kid in question. Nick knew everybody and their business. They were glad to share their news, good or bad. His was a friendly ear.

"Sure did! Going to be a Spartan!" High five.

At lunchtime that day Nick filled a grocery sack with

doubles of cheese rolls, chocolate milk and apples. The kids in the line teased him about his appetite, but the lunch lady just smiled. She knew.

Instead of going into the caf, he turned toward the exit. He liked to take a walk outside while he ate. Sure enough, there he was.

"Hey there, my man! Wanna come for a walk with me today?"

"I guess. Yeah."

Joseph Mack didn't usually eat at school. He told himself if he didn't eat, he wouldn't have to use the boys room. No way was he going to take a shit in there. He'd skip school and walk home first. Made that mistake just one time, in middle school. Got beat up. Went home bullied and bruised and then he got beat up some more.

"Stand up for yourself!" Ma insisted. No, she was not going to call the office and admit to some suit that her boy was unable to take a god-given crap without getting beat up by some assholes who thought they were better than her son.

Besides, he didn't often have money to eat. It was a cash-free system, where kids and staff all had barcodes on their ID tags, scanned to cover their fees from online accounts. Only parents could access those accounts and his mom was too busy to log in.

As they walked across the parking lot, Nick opened the bag for Joe. "Here. Eat."

They strode munching huge gooey cheese rolls. Pure carbs. Good fuel for active teenagers.

"Thanks."

"You got it."

They walked in silence. The early spring day was chilly but neither wore coats.

"I know it was you that called the hotline the other day. You did a good thing. People could've got hurt. Can you tell me about that note you found?"

"Um, it was on the bus. On the floor, by my seat. I picked it up because, you know, notes can be fun."

"Sure, like notes from girls? Hah!"

"Yeah!" Relieved.

"So you didn't write it yourself, right?"

Silence, Chewing. Swallowing.

"But you could tell me if you did, right?"

"Yeah. No. Sure."

They had circled the south lot and headed back to the building, chomping into apples.

"Okay, kid. Get to class."

"Thanks, Nick. See ya."

All his instincts knew that this hungry fifteen-year-old had written a threat to shoot up the school and reported it because if nobody found it, he would have felt compelled to carry out the threat. Lordy.

Weeks ago

People are always accusing others of doing things just for attention, as if that weren't a perfectly good reason to do things.

Yes, Joe's threat was a plea for attention. Little did his teachers or even Nick know that school was his safe place. Any bullying that took place there was a birthday party compared to what took place at home.

Gloria Mack oozed resentment from every pore.

The Macks lived outside of town on the only dirt road left in the township. She had grown up in the small house which was all her parents had to leave to her. She moved back home, young and pregnant, abandoned by her dying parents and a boyfriend who had other plans. None of that was her fault, but she had been stuck with all the responsibilities. With no support system, she had been unable to find work when Baby Joseph came along. It wasn't until he was into middle school that she found part time janitorial at the truck stop.

At thirty she was already used up. Used up and pissed off. None of it had been her fault. Is sadistic neglect a thing? She had never locked her son up or chained him to a bed, so she would never have admitted to abuse. She had left him in the car while she went to the bar, but that was only before he was able to unlock the door and let himself out. She plainly ignored his existence most of the time, never buying enough food for the two of them, and recognizing his existence only when it caused her inconvenience or embarrassment. Like any time the school called to report incidents of bullying. She refused meetings with the suits, and didn't go to the door when the social worker came calling. Any communication from the school was unwelcome, and justified diatribes against her son.

The same driver had been working that school bus route since Joe was in kindergarten. Most parents came out to see their small children get on the bus and meet them upon return. At the Mack's place there was never any sign of parents at all. The door was always closed. The curtains were always drawn. As the years passed, Joe grew from the wisp of a child to a sullen teenager. There was no bullying on her bus. She would not have it. She greeted each rider headed to or from school with a smile and, at holidays, a cookie. Between runs she checked her bus of debris and kept it swept clean. She shook her feelings of regret when, after she dropped him off at home, Joe trudged up the dirt driveway to the sad little house.

Joe had no friends at school except for Nick, but hanging around as Nick greeted all the other guys gave him a sense of society. Another guy who was always quiet and always alone was the tall senior who wore an army jacket and black hat. They never spoke, but once in a while Joe followed him out after school. One day he had followed him all the way downtown to the bakery, where he bought a carrot muffin and ignored the younger kid who had entered behind him. That smug black kid had been watching them from behind his laptop.

"What'choo lookin' at, asshole."

"Not much."

"Let's get outta here, asshole."

Outside on the sidewalk.

"What was that all about, man? Why have you been following me?"

"Sorry. I just didn't feel like riding the cheese wagon today. Are you walking home?"

And he was. So John and Joe began the long quiet walk to their dirt road west of town.

Check this out

When Daric arrived for the writing class, he noticed Linda had changed her seat, moving closer to him in a chair that had always been vacant. He noticed, but he did not respond.

The others arrived. The bell rang. Class commenced. It was not Friday, so the Author's Chair remained in its corner.

Ms Miller had a new lesson she was eager to try out. Sometimes they resulted in good learning experiences; sometimes they crashed and burned, but not so often these last couple years.

The theme for the day was Center of Attention. When her class looked squirmy, she pulled out a sheet and read something that she had composed. It was about a well known speech, told through the eyes of the person delivering the speech. It included what the crowd looked like and how they responded to his words. It included his thoughts when he paused for emphasis.

"You see," she explained, "the main character, for some reason, is the center of attention. How would that experience go?"

"Does it have to be true?" Linda asked.

"You get to make it up, but try to make it believable."

"But it can be make believe, right? Like the explorer in a cooking pot surrounded by African savages?"

People glanced nervously at Daric. Was he offended? He showed no reaction at all.

"Well, that's kind of silly, don't you think? Have it take place somewhere you know, but the event that brings attention could be either a good thing, like a performance or a celebration, or an unhappy thing, like an accident. Use your imagination about how it would feel to be in the center of attention."

The laptops opened.

Odd Man Out

When everyone's skin looks different than yours, you stand out in the crowd. When you walk into a room, people look and turn away to whisper to their friend. Then they turn back and smile at you and sometimes they say, "Hey, I really liked Barack Obama."

Sure, I think, and greens and Kanye.

Before my family moved here, I was just another black face in the crowd at a good school. It's easy to hide when your skin doesn't scream, "hey look at me!

42

I'm different!" Here I watch you and your friends together, and I see who is the leader and who are the posse. Default is so easy, but you do have to work harder to grow your character, when you are not being scrutinized every minute of the day, or made into the spokesman for an entire race.

Relax, White People. I am not here to judge you.

You don't have to convince me you are one of the good ones. Of course you are. Don't pity me because I am Black. I'm used to it, you know? And if you think I got into college because of some quota, don't even go there. NYC snapped me up because of my perfect SAT.

I just need to finish up a couple credits and then I'll be gone.

Fifteen minutes later Ms Miller asked them to swap with a partner for reading and reaction.

Linda looked hopefully at Daric. He shrugged and they switched laptops.

The house was always a busy place, but this time Dad would be home for the first time in three days, and Mom was fussing like it had been a year. All the sheets got changed and the laundry got done. The carpets were vacuumed and the kitchen floor was shiny with wax. She had cut fresh roses from the yard to put in a vase. Two teenage daughters mostly worked to stay out of their mom's way. They would be glad to see their father who would probably be generous handing out allowances, but they were skilled in avoiding housework, and it seemed to them the best way was escaping to the backyard in shorts and bathing suits to work on their tans. They took their books and phones with them. It was my turn to clean our bathroom. What a pigsty! Dirty towels and piles of discarded clothes had already gone down for the wash. The sink and the shower and the floor were gross. I grabbed my toothbrush and headed out the front door.

Nobody noticed that I was gone.

Linda had been sucked into a black hole. Oh this poor child.

She beat the after school crowd to the bakery and chose a table near the wall and opened her laptop. This was her new favorite place to write, now that she knew who else had discovered it. With every tinkle of the bell she glanced up at the arrivals. Within fifteen minutes he entered. It seemed he had a favorite table, in the middle, which the others avoided. Respect.

Daric ordered a coffee, black, and Linda sighed. He opened is own laptop, oblivious to the young lady crushing just a few feet away. She slipped a phone from her pocket and angled it in his direction. A photo for luck.

John and Joe fell into the habit of walking home together after that. Eventually they spoke. Eventually John talked about the legacy his father had left him, about the Marines and the handguns in the safe deposit box. He knew he was bragging about his dad, something he had never really done, but Joe seemed interested. When he finally asked about Joe's own father, the conversation stopped. Then Joe confided his secret.

"It was me that found that threat at school."

"Really? It was a real good thing you called it in. You got us a day off."

Joe couldn't tell if his companion was making fun of him.

"Well, the note was on the bus, you know? On the floor. I picked it up on the way home. I guess I could have given it to the driver, but at first I didn't even think it was real, you know?" He did not have the memory of a brave father, but he did have a story.

"Then after I got home and was thinking about it, I was all 'somebody needs to know about this,' you know? They tell us see something, say something. So I called the hotline. I didn't tell my mom about it. She wouldn't'a let me call. She'd'a just ripped up that note."

John had nothing to say about that.

They reached John's drive first.

"See ya."

"Yep."

Jan's laptop was opened to Google Classroom to read the week's journal entries. John's included a heading: Fiction

> Joey had a seat to himself on the bus ride home. His stop was one of the last. The bus bumped over the train tracks and jolted to a stop. His backpack fell to the floor. He reached under the seat to grab the pack when he felt a folded piece of paper. He picked it up along with the bag. It was folded in a weird way. He jammed the paper into his pocket as he got up to leave.
>
> "Bye, Joey. See you Monday," said Molly, the driver.
>
> After the bus moved on down the road, Joey pulled out the piece of paper and unfolded it. It read:

Somebody should just shoot up that dam school.

It was printed in pencil. He put it into his backpack and walked up the driveway and into the house.

He thought about it after dinner and again the next morning. On Saturday while his mom was out, he found the flyer from school with the hotline phone number on it. He called it and told about the note. He was not sure what would happen next.

Despite the fiction label at the top, Jan was quite sure John knew something about the threat that had shut down their school. Surely he knew she would tell somebody about this. She had to. She commented on the page, "thank you, John, for this information. I will see that it gets to the right person."

Monday morning she dropped by the boiler room with two cups of coffee in to-go cups.

"Nick? You here?"

"I sure am," he answered. "What's up so early on this Monday morning?"

"I need to show you something." She offered him a cup, and pulled the laptop out of her bag.

"Does this sound legitimate to you? I don't want to take it to White until you see it."

It was consistent with Joe's account of the event.

"Why don't you wait on it just a bit. Say until this

afternoon. Let me check on something first."

Someone arriving at the school at lunch time might have noticed two people strolling the perimeter of the parking lot, munching cheese rolls and talking. Joey admitted that there never was a note at all, and that he just called the hotline on his own. He felt bad that it caused a lot of trouble and also that he had lied to his friend John.

"You know we need to go talk to Mr. White about this," said Nick softly.

"Everybody's going to be mad at me," said Joey.

"Well, what you did could've got somebody hurt."

"I just wanted to do something," the kid muttered. "I never get to do things. I thought it would be cool. My mom is going to be so mad. She's always mad at me." His face turned red and his eyes got wet.

"Let's finish our lunch and you go on to class. When Mr. White sends for you, I'll help explain what happened."

The house was empty when Joey came in. It was better when she was out. The boss at the truck stop had offered Gloria the chance to fill in for a waitress who often missed her shift, so that afternoon she went in early. The waitress hourly was less than cleaning, but there would be tips. At least that was the excuse. She figured if she could pick up extra hours waiting table, she could still do her cleaning shift after and maybe get ahead for once. Never having waited table, she was not prepared for how tired she would be at the end of the shift. Still, she cleaned the kitchen and the dining room and the rest rooms, before stumbling home after midnight.

The house was dark and quiet.

Thursday after school John stopped by the bank to get into the safe deposit box. He opened the heavy box and removed the handguns, turning each one over in his hands, fingering the triggers. He had no ammo for any of them, but that was for later. Now he hoped his Dad could help him know which one would be the best for him. He could take all four to the range. Try them all out. Decide, and then return the others to the bank for safe storage. The backpack was much heavier when he left. The walk to the range proved to be a workout.

Entry to the range was members only. He carried a key card in his wallet that let him in.

"Hey, Chuck!" He addressed the owner of the private range. He had not seen Chuck since his father's funeral.

"Well, good to see you, buddy! What are you up to today? Going to shoot?"

"Yes I am. I figured you could help me with something." He set the backpack on a bench and opened it.

"Dad left these for me. Maybe you've seen them already, but he didn't usually keep them at home. I want to get my CPL. I'm not sure which I want to use, so I'd like to try them out. Can you set me up with some ammo?"

"Sure we can do that, son. You can use the range, but you'll have to wait until you're 21 to get a CPL. State law. When the time comes, you'll think about how you'll want to wear your firearm. On the chest, on the belt. What will impede your movement the least but still be accessible. I run a holster class for that if you are interested. You'll need to take the CPL class and register at the county clerk's office. There's a fee, but your dad taught you about safety and respect for the firearm and about range etiquette. I doubt you'll have any problem."

He reached into a cabinet and produced a box of fifty standard pressure .38 Special cartridges.

"That revolver you got there holds five cartridges. Start with these and then you can try out the semis. Let's go into the range and I'll show you how to load it."

John was grateful to be the only shooter in the range. He wanted to do his dad proud and not look like a doofus in front of strangers.

Two hours later he had tried them all and decided he preferred the Glock. It sat well in his grip, and he had better accuracy with it, although that would certainly improve with more practice, whichever pistol he chose. He pulled out his wallet to pay for the cartridges, but Chuck refused his money.

"The first box is on me in tribute to your father. I am glad that you will continue the family tradition. If you plan to come in regular to shoot, why don't you keep your handguns here? There are some lockers the other members use, and I can lend you a padlock to protect your property. I'd hate for you to have trouble carting those firearms around in your backpack.

"Thanks, Chuck. I appreciate your time. That's a good idea.".

"Hey there, Mike! You going to shoot today?" Chuck was looking over John's shoulder toward the open door. When John turned he recognized the old Marine from the bakery.

"Don't know if you've met this young man," Chuck said. "This is Marcus's kid, John. Looks like he will be putting in some time in the range, just like his old man.

John, this is Mike Knott."

The two shook hands.

"I knew your dad a long time ago," the old Marine said. "Had him in class when he was a kid. Good kid. Always showed his work." He chuckled.

John did not know what to say to that, but he enjoyed being treated like he was grown. The shooting range was his new favorite spot.

"Hey! I've got to get home for dinner," said John. "I spent longer here than I thought."

Next afternoon he walked home with Joey and mentioned he would be heading over to the range. He asked the younger kid if he wanted to come along.

"Really? That would be so cool."

Immediately John regretted the invitation. He felt like a babysitter. But he had not mentioned the guns to anybody else, and Joe was pretty easy to impress. "Okay. Let's turn here. It's close."

The range was housed in a windowless building half mile off the road, easy to miss if you didn't know about it. Joey was enthusiastic about everything. The keycard. That the guy in charge was cool. An old guy exited the range itself to the locker area, pulling off his goggles and ear protection.

"Hey, it's my Marine buddy! Good to see you!"

"Hey. Joe here is hangin' out this afternoon. Joey, this is Mr. Knott. He was in the Marines like my dad. Marines stick together, he says."

"We sure do. You boys going to shoot?"

"If it's okay with Chuck."

He selected the Glock. Joe picked up the Smith&Wesson.

"Do you think I could shoot this one?"

"I guess we'll find out."

He looked around for Chuck to get some cartridges.

Chuck was annoyed that John had brought a buddy along. That afternoon the range was not busy, but members liked their privacy, not being gawked at by underaged kids who did not know what they were doing. He spoke about it to John while he pulled a box of cartridges from the cabinet.

"In case your father never told you, I'm pretty anal about rules, and the rule is under-18 needs to be accompanied by a parent. If he wants, he can bring his mom or dad in and sign up for lessons. He can watch from the break room, but he can't come into the range. And today you buy your own ammo."

"Okay. Yeah, well, he doesn't have a dad and his mom works afternoons and nights so it probably won't happen, but I'll let him know."

No other members were using the range at the time. Bill Knott sat in the small lounge with a cup of coffee. He nodded to Joey. They watched the range through a window.

"So, young man, you're not shooting today after all."

"Naw. If you're not eighteen you gotta have your mom or dad with you."

"Next time you'll want to bring one of them with you, eh?"

"No shooting for me then. Mom works all the time. I got no dad."

"Want a Mt. Dew? I'm buyin'. Everybody's got a dad. Did yours die?"

"Thanks." Joey popped the tab and took a long drink. "I don't know what happened to him. Mom never said, but

I think she's still mad at him. Sure acts mad at somebody."

Muffled gunshots from the range. Good sound proofing. He thought it would be louder. Looked like John was a pretty good shot. The paper target was getting raggedy where some guy's chest would be. Each shot exploded with a flash of fire. So cool.

"What's your name, kid? I'm Mike Knott. You can call me Mr. Knott." He grinned at his own joke.

"Joe."

"Well, Joe, I like to come down here to shoot couple afternoons a week. Gets kinda boring by yourself."

"I guess."

"Do you think it would be okay with your ma if I gave you some range training? Chuck would be okay with it if she wrote you a note."

The offer took Joey by surprise. The old guy didn't look like a weirdo, but you never know.

"Maybe. I don't know."

John would know what to do. It would be pretty cool if they both could come shoot after school.

"I'll talk to my mom. Thanks for the Dew."

And he did. He sat up waiting for her when she came in after cleaning the truck stop.

"Thought you would be asleep by now."

"I waited for you. Got something I want to ask you about."

She kicked off her shoes and plopped down on the couch. She sighed. "What is it now?"

"There's this old guy around town. You probably saw him before. He used to be a Marine in Nam. I was talking to him today at the shooting range."

"You need to come right home from school. Nobody

needs you hanging out at that shooting range."

"Well, John is my friend. I don't think you know him but he lives down the road from us and sometimes we walk home together. Anyway, he got some guns that were his dad's and he's learning how to shoot them. And Mr. Knott said if it was okay with you, he could teach me how to shoot too. It would be really fun to learn. And then I can protect you and our home. I mean, some day if I ever get a gun."

"Mr. Knott? You met Mr. Knott? He was my teacher when I was in the sixth grade. He was crazy and scary. He never scared me, but he was big and loud."

Joey was disappointed The guy didn't seem crazy and scary to him. Looked like it was going to be a no.

She looked at her disappointed son. "Tell you what," she said, "Let me talk to John's mom. We work together. Did you know that? John is going to be there at the range too, right?"

Mr. Knott had been quite a character back in the day, but actually the kids in his class had liked him very much. He pretended to be tough, but she suspected he never hit anybody with that damn paddle.

"Are you sure you're old enough to learn how to shoot?"

"Yes, but they have a rule that you have to have your parent's permission if you're under 18."

She liked the idea of her son being able to stand up for himself. If anybody could grow the kid a pair, it was Mike Knott.

A couple afternoons later Mr. Knott and his new friend Joe met up to begin training in handgun safety.

Meanwhile

The head of security stopped by the principal's office after lunch.

"Got a minute, boss?"

"Sure. You heard something?"

The door closed, muffling their voices. When Nick emerged they had agreed that the warning had been a hoax and that no good would be achieved by involving the police. The perpetrator would receive some extra attention from support personnel. And cheese roll therapy. Nick reported variations of the decision to Jan and to Joe. Didn't want the kid distracted all week waiting to be summoned to the office.

Later

Linda beat the after school crowd to the bakery. She chose a table near the wall and opened her laptop. She had a new writing prompt, and if only she had taken it to heart.

Stop right there.

But no. Before thinking about her next story, she idly went to her Instagram account and posted the picture of her love in a frame of hearts.

Ms Miller had told them to fit that phrase someplace into the story. It could be a direct quote. It could be part of a bigger sentence. It could come at the beginning to kick the action off, or it could come at the end. She thought about the afternoon when she had first thought about leaving home. Mom had stopped her before she got to the end of the block. That was good for a story. Write what you know, right?

On the other side of the coffee shop, three girls leaned

in to look at a phone screen and started to snicker. They glanced over, past the good looking black guy in the center to where Linda hunched over her keyboard. This was going to be good.

Linda quickly acquired two new followers, and by dinner time would have dozens more.

Daric was marginally aware of the girls, but found them easy to ignore. He was in the middle of a story of his own that he wanted to finish before moving on to the current prompt. He was actually enjoying the writing class more than he thought he would.

Same Time

After school, Charley headed to the range for his weekly practice. You couldn't tell from the parking lot, but the place was clearly booming. He didn't mind shooting around other people because with his hearing protection on, it was easy to ignore them. He avoided, however, sharing the range with beginners. Accidents could happen to anyone. He stopped at his locker to grab a box of cartridges and looked through the window to see who was shooting today. If Thursdays became too popular, he would consider switching his routine. He recognized John Kerr and town legend, Mike Knott. There was another kid next to Knott. He'd seen him around school. He'd just as soon keep his shooting to himself. It was a small enough town that he didn't need all of his business shared around school. What happened at the faculty meeting was bad enough. He stashed the cartridges back into the locker and left.

After spending most of the hour blasting holes in a paper target, John stepped out into the break room. Chuck had been restocking the fridge with cold drinks.

"If you want one, just put a dollar here inside the door and help yourself. The money goes to the pet shelter. You know I'm a softie for dogs, right?"

John pulled a bill out of his wallet and reached for a Mountain Dew.

"You must really miss your old man, amIright?"

"Oh yes I do. Hanging out with him was the best. I almost feel like he's here with me sometimes. I wish I could still talk to him."

"I know I'm not your father, John, but if you ever want to, you can talk to me."

"Right. Thanks. The thing is, before he died he asked me to take care of mom. To make sure she is safe. High school is nearly over and I don't know the best way to do that. Everybody else has plans for college. I can't go and just leave her. Dad would kill me."

Chuck nodded.

"Well, not everybody has to go to college. I skipped my own graduation and started work that day for the township police force. Of course, I had been part-timing for them for months so they knew me pretty good."

"Good point." John nodded. "Not everybody has to go, and some go that don't really want to. Seems that's all they talk about at school. Get good grades. Go to college."

"You don't really have to decide right this minute. I bet your dad will have your back no matter what you decide. The man didn't raise no fool."

John 's laugh burst out in a snort.

The load had been lifted from his shoulders, and the walk home more buoyant than in months.

Somewhere. Anywhere.
Gloria leaves Half Way.

Half Way in neon glowed through the dark, visible half mile down the interstate. One more big rig pulled off and headed into the backlot out behind the fuel pumps. The driver, a tall man with a dad bod climbed down, stretched, adjusted himself, and headed for a door marked Professional Drivers Only. He stopped to wash up a tad, then found a booth and glanced at the list of daily specials.

"I see him," Gloria said, and headed over with the coffee pot.

Marian had begun waiting table after finishing the day's baking. The tips were good. She and Gloria divided the area approximately in half. Marian waited on the families and civilians. Gloria had the drivers, nearly all men who tended to soften her hard edges with remarks, flirting. She seemed to like that sort of thing, and Marian was happy to clean up after toddlers in exchange. She wore the universal sign of a faithful widow: her man's gold wedding band on a necklace chain, outside her uniform. Suitors need not apply. Single moms are not all alike.

"Coffee for you, darlin'?"

Just a little sugar for the customer to help the tip.

"Yes, thanks." He waited while she poured. "What have you got tonight that's special? I mean good. To eat."

Dirty thoughts by one or both.

"The pork chops are wonderful. They come with potatoes plus another side."

"Great. Do that with American fries and some soup. Got vegetable beef?"

"Sure do. I'll get that first."

Trucker Travis watched the waitress walk away. Something he always enjoyed. Watching waitresses walk away.

Travis wasn't actually his name, but some buddies started calling him that for his choice of country music. Now it was his CB handle and ladies seemed to like it.

Gloria learned to like waiting table a lot better than cleaning, so when it was obvious to the boss that the other waitress needed firing, Gloria moved into it full time. Somebody else took up the after hours janitorial. She and Marian were friendly without becoming friends. They both had boys at the high school and no man at home, but that was about all they shared. Lately it turns out their sons were pals, walking home together most afternoons, and on Thursdays stopping at the gun range for target practice. So they were also neighbors. Not next door, but down the road neighbors. As Joe became a teenager, Gloria realized that she was still young enough to think about a future of her own. No place like the Half Way for meeting men.

She slicked on a little lipstick before heading back to the booth with a bowl of vegetable beef soup.

Someone should have told Gloria stop right there, but

no one did, and when Joey got up next morning, he was a little surprised to find that his ma had not come home. More relieved than worried, he wolfed down a bowl of cereal with the last of the milk and headed out the door.

She had been pregnant with her boy when she was his age, and managed just fine. She figured he would be just fine, too.

That afternoon Joey stopped at the mailbox. He was surprised to find two or three days worth of mail crammed in there. That's what finally clued him in that his mom had not been home for a while. He tossed the junk mail and catalogs into the trash and set what looked like bills on the kitchen counter. A check of the cupboard revealed that the grocery fairy had not visited. He was out of food. This situation was now troubling. He decided to walk down the road to John's house. Bet there would be food there.

And there was. When he opened the door, John was munching on a thick meatloaf sandwich.

"Ya got any more of that?"

"Sure we do. Come on in, Joe. What's up?"

He assembled a second sandwich and a glass of milk. Marian kept their fridge stocked.

"Is your mom at work now? At the Half Way? Could you call her?"

"If I got a good reason, I could."

"I haven't seen my mom for a couple days. I want to know if she is at work or what. I'm kinda gettin' worried."

John pulled out his cell and called. Marian answered. She said Gloria had not been in to work the past two days, and the boss was getting hot about it. If the boys found her, they should let her know she should call in.

Neither Joe nor Gloria had cell phones. The two boys decided maybe they should call the police and report her missing.

Of course adult women go away all the time. On vacation, to visit family or friends, to escape the dreariness of life. The officer took some information and said they would keep an eye out for her, but there would be no All Points Bulletin.

John's cell rang. His mother was calling back.

"Let Joey know he should stay with us for a while. We can't have that child staying home alone with no food in the house." The police would probably be contacting CPS. "And have him wash his clothes, for goodness sake. The kid probably reeks."

John agreed that was a fine idea. He found some sweats for Joey to put on and tossed a load into the wash.

When Joey settled onto the couch for the night, it occurred to him that if he were going to be living alone back home, he might need some protection. Maybe he would bring the borrowed revolver home tomorrow after shooting practice. The lessons were paying off. He felt more confident and his aim was pretty good.

He awoke to the smell of bacon. Breakfast sounds coming from the kitchen. John's mom was at the stove fixing bacon and eggs and toast. Joey stumbled into the kitchen.

"That sure smells good, ma'am. My mom doesn't believe in cooking."

"Oh you poor dear." She resisted the urge to sweep him into a hug. "Who wouldn't want to cook for such a good boy?"

Joe instantly fell in love.

She continued, "I want you to plan on staying with us until your mom gets back. There's plenty of space and cooking for two teenage boys is no more trouble than cooking for one." There was a spare room that she would fix up for him. He would have his own bedroom by the time he got home from school that day.

"Okay. That's really nice of you. Thanks, ma'am. I don't want to be any trouble."

"You would never be any trouble. But instead of ma'am, you could call me mom. I'll leave that up to you."

The morning sun streamed into the tidy kitchen. It would be okay.

So Over Valentines Day

"Linda 'n' Daric sittin' in a tree." Some refrains never die.

"So you really like him?" Sharon and Linda had been besties since elementary, just ask her. Of course Sharon had gone on to find other friends in high school, and the two did not talk like they once did, especially at school.

"Oh, I don't know. It won't go anywhere. I just think he's gorgeous is all."

"Well, girl, I don't think he's got a girlfriend, so you might as well move on it."

Linda made the turn into Ms Miller's room. She didn't see Daric following close behind.

"Um, Linda, we need to talk." That's never good to hear. "Do you know anything about the valentine I just found in my locker?"

He held the printout of her Instagram image.

"Oh...my...God."

She dropped her backpack.

"Girl, I am flattered to pieces by all the hearts, and it is a pretty cool pic, but you know that I am gone when school's out, right? I mean, I am not even staying for graduation."

Linda did not answer. Apparently this was all news to her. She fled the classroom. There was going to be some ugly crying.

Hundreds of miles away, Gloria excused herself to the ladies. "Just need to freshen up a bit."

They had stopped for breakfast at yet another truck stop, a couple states to the west. She washed her face and brushed her teeth. She longed for a hot shower and to wash her hair. Instead she did her makeup and practiced a smile. She emerged to the dining room and scanned the early crowd. Maybe he had returned to the rig. She walked back out to the lot. The space where Travis's semi had been parked was empty. She returned to the dining room and took a booth nearest the window.

"Just a coffee, please."

He was different. He would be back. She was sure of it. Two cups later, she realized she ought to be making a plan. Nine hundred miles from home. She looked around for the boss. That was obviously him at the register. She wandered over.

She gave him her best waitress smile. "Hey there, you hiring?"

Spring Breaking

"When you are feeling disappointed, is there something that will usually cheer you up? Say you were planning a long hike or bike ride with a group of friends, and the day's weather was just wet and miserable. You and your friends can't keep your plans. What happens?"

Sam, who did not usually join class discussions, suggested the obvious. "We would figure out something else to do that day. Go to a movie or the arcade. No biggie."

Heads nodded.

"Okay, how about a more individual disappointment. Your family has a birthday tradition. The birthday kid goes out to breakfast with either your mom or you dad. Just the two of you. No siblings. If the birthday is on a school day, you take a note from home. Maybe you miss first hour. You've been doing this since you were little, and now that you are nearly adults, the chance for coffee and conversation is even more special."

The teenagers in front of her were getting into this. They liked family traditions and this one was obviously a winner.

"But on your birthday, your younger brother wakes up with a high fever. He's really sick. Dad has left for work and Mom needs to take the sick child to the doctor. She explains. You get it. But you are still disappointed. How do you deal?"

"Well, my little brother would be more important than birthday breakfast. I would claim a raincheck on that and offer to go along to the doctor. Still get my first hour pass, you know what I mean?"

That got a laugh. For Sam, the birthday bonus would be missing first hour, not breakfast out with Mother Superior.

"Today's assignment deals with coping with disappointment. You are writing fiction, remember, so it does not need to be autobiographical, but all writers draw on experiences they have had or they witness."

They looked thoughtful as they flipped open their laptops. So many disappointments to choose from, thought Jan.

"Does it matter how long it is?" Linda asked.

"You could probably put together this kind of scene in three-to-four hundred words. Include clues to time and place. Let your characters speak and act."

Daric glanced over at Linda. She would never dare read it on author's day, but he had a pretty good idea he would have a starring role in this particular disappointment.

Linda did not look up. She was already hard at work.

After the "disappointing" writing class, John left the building by a different route. He swung by the chem lab hoping to catch Mr. Keyes before he left. The teacher was busy with a student and John lingered at a distance until the two were finished. Then he approached. He had taken chemistry last year, but it wasn't AP and it was with another teacher. Mr. Keyes wondered why the visit.

"You don't really know me, like maybe not at all, but I am hoping you can do me a big favor," John began.

Charley waited for him to go on.

"We shoot at the same range."

Charley busied himself straightening his desk. His secret was out. How much did this kid know?

"Well, I go in there to shoot on Thursdays after school. Chuck gave me a locker so I don't have to carry my firearm. That was really nice of him, and I appreciate it, but I have this range bag that I need to take. It won't fit in the locker, and I don't want to bring it into school. You know how that could get crazy, right? So I was hoping you could help me figure out what to do with it, just on Thursdays."

Charley smiled at the earnest young man in front of him. Sounded like they were both private about their hobby.

"What's your name?"

The kid told him.

"I have some space in my closet here, which is kept locked all day. If you want, you could get your range bag in here first thing Thursday morning, before first hour, and it would stay there until you need it that afternoon."

"That would work great for me, if it is not a big inconvenience for you. Thank you."

Well, That's Disappointing

"Jane and Sarah had been friends since second grade playing Four Square at recess. Recess was their favorite time of day, when Sarah flirted with the boys until they chased her and she ran until they caught her, all of them shrieking with laughter. Not Jane, though. It was not ladylike to be chasing boys, even then, and Jane knew that was exactly what her best friend was doing. She merely watched with an expression of embarrassment and joined the line back to class when the bell rang.

By middle school Sarah was going with a boy, although they did not actually go anywhere. They talked at school between classes. The girls still sat together for lunch. Too bad recess was a thing of the past. In high school the friends drifted apart, as often happens.

Just too many boys, and none of them seemed very interested in Jane. They were interested in Sarah, who no longer had to chase them. They were chasing her.

Jane tried her hand at writing poetry because she could express her feelings without worrying about topic sentences and supporting examples. It was one place where she felt free of all the rules.

As much as she poured her heart into her poetry, she would never in a million years let anybody else read them. Her feelings were private. That was until her best childhood friend outed her on Instagram. And none of the boys seemed very interested in Jane."

"Oh, cry me a river," said John with a snort.

Daric straightened in his chair. The betrayal by a friend was nothing to laugh about. Everyone in the class knew about the "valentine" someone had planted in his locker. That someone was probably cold-hearted 'Sarah'. And everyone had watched Linda bolt from the room that day, tears streaming. Crying a river, indeed.

Author's Day had become therapy day.

"There's time for one more today." Ms Miller was surprised when John assumed the chair just vacated by

Linda.

Daric whispered to Linda as she returned to her usual seat.

"You are braver than that bitch who stabbed you in the back online."

Linda had begun trembling.

John leaned back in the chair and flipped open his laptop. He began to read.

> "Run 'n' shoot sounded like a basketball drill, but this didn't happen in the gym. It is one of the advanced classes offered at the gun range. After a man is a pretty good target shooter, and after he passes the holster class, he can sign up for run 'n' shoot.
>
> I was looking forward to doing that. It sounded fun, like a sport. Finally there would be an advantage to using my father's Glock 9."

Feet shuffled. The students were not the only ones curious, nervous. Jan recalled the clench in her gut during the lockdown drill.

> "Dad and I were shooting buddies. We hunted together, and when I was old enough, he took me with him to the range. It wasn't until after he died that I discovered

he had handguns in a safe deposit box. That was where I found the Glock. I have been taking lessons for the past few months. I have a holster that I keep in a locker at the range, because I only use it there until I am 21 and old enough for CPL. Most people don't know about all the gun laws there are.

I signed up to learn run 'n' shoot. It's about self defense against three opponents. The bad guys are represented by three targets. A blank target on each side represents a barrier, like a car door or the corner of a building.

The shooter starts on one side, say the left, pulls his pistol from his holster and makes it hot, and then runs across to the opposite side, shooting twice at each target as he goes. On the other side, he reloads and runs back, again firing twice at each target. This is timed and checked for accuracy. A shot that misses the target's stop zone adds .2 second to your time. It's harder than it sounds, but it's also a good stress reliever.

I was not disappointed."

He closed his laptop and looked around. His audience was rapt. Daric leaned forward on his desk, hands covering his eyes. His sigh was audible across the room.

"Man, why'd you have to go and do that?"

"Do what?"

The bell sounded the end of the school day. Most lingered.

"Hey, I get it. My whole family shoots," said Sam. "It's cool."

Imagining that another student could possibly have a handgun in his backpack reignited the anxiety that had almost faded.

Daric shook his head and slung his backpack over his shoulder.

"You da man." He headed for the door.

John muttered, grabbed his own bag and left.

"Asshole."

She's Back

The afternoon shift at the HalfWay hid their surprise when Gloria strolled in with a trucker that Thursday. She had hitched a ride in a rig headed east and convinced the driver that for Marian's pie he would not regret the stop. Instead of joining the driver in a booth, she headed into the kitchen in search of pie and the boss.

"Hello, Marian. I hope we're not out of pie. I promised my ride he would not be disappointed. Hi, Boss. Is it okay if I still call you that? I would love to get my job back. Any job, actually. You know, this girl is just not made for life on the road. What d'ya say?"

"He's in luck. We still have two slices of blueberry in the case."

Boss scoffed, turned red in the face, and pivoted into the cooler.

He'd need some time to consider. Maybe cooling off so as not to wring her neck.

She plated two slices of pie, checked the coffee pot, and turned toward the dining room.

"Marian, tell Boss I'll call him later after he's had time to cool down. I need to go home and say hello to my kid."

"Your kid's name is Joe, in case you forgot. I know it's been a while. What? Three months? And he's been living at my house, just so you know. You really have a helluva nerve, Gloria. You do not deserve that sweet child."

"I am just gonna get in my car and go find my son."

Could she thank Marian for taking the kid in? Maybe later. For now she had all the smack talk she could stand.

"Since it's Thursday, he will be with my boy John. They're at the range."

Gloria looked confused.

"The gun range."

What the hell? Then she remembered the permission note she had written. The car started on the second try and she pulled out of the lot and headed toward town.

The range looked more remote than it really was, about half mile down from her own house, set back off the road, down a dirt drive and surrounded by trees. Unless you were looking for it, you'd never know it was there. A discreet sign. Two cars and a flashy pickup truck were parked outside. She pulled in next to the truck, got out and headed for the door. "Members Only." Electronic keypad. No windows. She pounded on the metal door with her fist.

Surveillance cameras showed the fear and rage on her face. It was a look Joe knew.

Chuck, John and Mr. Knott were all still in the range itself and wearing ear protection. Over the loud shots, they had not heard the banging on the door. Joe only heard it on his way back from the bathroom. He knew he would have to face her sooner or later, so it might as well be now. He opened the door and stepped outside.

"Oh, Joey honey, I was so worried about you." She pulled him into a hug which confused him.

"Where did you go, Ma? I was worried. I thought you

were dead. I called the police. I didn't know what to do."

"Oh, I know, honey. It won't ever happen again, I swear. I just needed to get away for a little while. But now I'm back and we can go home and everything will be okay."

"Maybe. But I don't live there anymore. I live with my friend John and his mom now. I have my own room. They have breakfast and dinner together every day."

He pulled out of the hug and turned back toward the closed door.

He had no key card to open it. He could still hear the thump of bullets.

"I am glad they took you in, but that was only temporary, you know. Now it's time for us to get home. I need to cook some dinner for my boy."

She grabbed his arm and pulled him toward the car.

"No, Ma. I'm not going with you. There's no food in the house anyway. You'd better go get some groceries. I need to get back inside. Mr. Knott will be looking for me."

Gloria pulled back her fist to convince her recalcitrant child.

"Stop right there."

The old Marine filled the doorway, a pistol hung from his hand. Joe recalled his words: always presume the gun to be loaded.

The gun is loaded.

"Please, Ma, just go home. Or go get some food and then go home."

John appeared in the doorway, just behind the old man. He was concerned but unafraid.

Inside, Chuck was calling 911.

Frustrated and outmanned, Gloria got in her car and

slammed the door. It took two tries to start and she drove away in a cloud of dust.

Joe felt tears starting and he blinked them back.

Bill Knott ejected his empty magazine. This time the gun had not been loaded. He knew better than to just walk around with a loaded gun when he did not plan to shoot it.

Two police units pulled down the dusty drive. They would not be needed today.

"This would be so good for Author's Day."

That was John.

Rites of Spring

It was spring. Talk had been buzzing for weeks about prom. Seems that someone had slipped up and failed to reserve the venue that had been used for a number of years, and early in the semester a rumor circulated that prom was canceled. The reaction, predictably, was rage.

Then David Shrubs, the marketing teacher proposed an idea to the junior class advisers, and they thought it just might work. So during Spring Break they leaked the rumor that prom had been rescued, and that it would be held in the high school gym. The reaction, again predictably, was more rage. Some of the seniors complained that the juniors had failed in their fundraising efforts; no one was speaking to the Junior Class president. Mr. Shrubs summoned the prom committee to a quick meeting and shared his vision: instead of streamers and balloons, they would transform the gym end of the building into a completely different place. It would be amazing. All they needed to do was trust him and show up when he needed their help. Seeing no other options, they quickly agreed.

Shrubs had connections and creative people across the country who owed him favors. The rest of the faculty was intrigued. Something interesting was afoot and they all wanted in on it.

The following Friday a huge bundle was delivered to the school. Shrubs called on the committee. After hours, when everyone else had gone home, they unpacked vast sheets of camouflage fabric that had been the backdrop last year for a dinosaur exhibit at the science museum in a nearby town. This draped the ceiling and walls of the gym. The ceiling lights, bleachers and basketball rims vanished. After Monday morning's first hour gym class: "I hear the prom theme is Vietnam."

Groans, but not rage.

Shrubs commandeered the semi trailer used for band equipment storage during the fall competition season. He hid props and packages there and it filled over the next few weeks. Then he started filling up the field house with risers that had been borrowed from church and school choirs across the county. An outrigger dugout canoe and palm trees from the old South Pacific movie set were shipped in from California. It turned out that the hockey coach's brother in law drove truck, and just added those items to his load.

Later that week the seniors received their prom invitations: a large pink hibiscus with text in elaborate calligraphy. "The Junior Class invites you to A Night To Remember"

The quickest to Google produced the reference to the 1958 movie about the sinking of the Titanic. Shrieks like from steerage. Around the corner in the marketing room, Dave Shrubs tried not to laugh.

That day after school he met with a group of dads and granddads who figured that cleaning up the school's courtyard would be a good job for them. After clearing out the overgrown vegetation and trash and pruning the trees, they planted flowering shrubs and added a small reflective pond, lights, and potted flowers. The prom guests would be able to step outside for air without wandering off.

Linda was a junior and had offered to help the prom committee, so when speculation broke out in Creative Writing, the others turned to her for the inside scoop. She smiled and shrugged. She really did not know what the big plan was. She simply would show up to help when the committee was summoned and do what she was told.

"You mean the committee doesn't even know what it is doing? This is going to be a mess!"

"We really should just trust Mr. Shrubs. He says not to worry and it's going to be the best prom ever." Linda tried her best to be positive.

Daric turned to Linda. "You know, I had planned to give prom a miss, but I gotta see this. How about it, Linda? Do you have a date yet?"

Had she heard him right?

She faced him. "Are you asking me to prom?"

"I suppose I am."

"Well, okay."

The following week ten teachers found packages in their mailboxes. Jan and Charley had both offered their help with prom, figuring it would be as chaperones. The packages contained colorful Hawaiian shirts and their assignment: valet parking.

Three girls getting ready for prom puts a real strain on the bathroom.

Linda was the middle kid. Older sister Charlotte had

been going to prom since tenth grade. She always had an older boyfriend. Now she was the senior, and Ray had come home from college to take her to her last high school prom. Younger sister Sheila was in 10th grade. This was her first prom, as it was Linda's. They took their cues from the glamorous Charlotte. They also wore her prom dresses. Sheila had wanted the strapless silver one, but realized Linda, by seniority, should get first pick. Linda, the peacemaker, let Sheila wear the silver. It suited her, and she already had the figure to hold it up. She would wear the more modest pink dress.

The three giddy girls came home from the hairdresser and headed to the bathroom for the makeup ritual. Linda hated the eyeliner, but the others insisted it was mandatory. She gave in and hoped there would be no crying. Daric had already seen enough of that, and adding eyeliner mess?

No way.

The doorbell rang. Ray let himself in and greeted Mr and Mrs. Johnson, who asked about his classes as if they really cared. The bell rang again for Sheila's date, a quiet senior boy none of them had ever noticed before. When he first spotted his date in the stunning silver, he looked like a first time lottery winner, which is just what she had been hoping for.

The doorbell rang for the third arrival, and Linda's mom left the young man standing on the porch. She flurried into the girls' room.

"Linda? There is a black man on the porch, and he's asking for you."

"Jeez, Mom. Just have him come in. That's Daric."

"I just don't know about this. I need to talk to your father."

"Well, talk all you want after we leave. Daric is a nice friend from school and we are going to prom." She felt confidant. Could it have been the eyeliner?

Mrs. Johnson returned to the foyer and opened the door for Daric who had the manners to pretend he had not just been insulted. He greeted both of Linda's parents and the other two young men, then the sisters. The foyer was crowded. He looked stunning in a black tux. When Linda entered, his face broke into a wide smile.

"You are beautiful. Sorry, guys, but I am the winner tonight."

Linda blushed as pink as her dress, took his arm, and headed out the door. No stopping for parental caution or photographs.

Prom night was balmy. Two rotating searchlights pierced the sky, and cars lined the streets in all directions for nearly a mile. Curious adults, parents and neighbors had been let in early to check out the transformation of an ordinary high school into a Polynesian nightclub. The entrance was a softly lit grotto of boulders and lush tropical plants. Inside, a volcano flowed glowing lava. The dance floor was in the middle, under a wide inverted umbrella filled with flowers and twinkle lights. Risers created levels for the round tables and chairs. After the adults were shooed out, they lingered to watch the glamorous arrivals step out of their vehicles and be announced over a loudspeaker.

"Ladies and gentlemen, Miss Linda Johnson and Mr. Daric Richardson."

The crowd murmured at the attractive couple, and Linda savored a new confidence as she took Daric's arm and walked up the red carpet. It was the first time he had seen her smile.

The night was full of happy chatter and dancing, just as prom should be.

No one complained about the venue, but one young man was overheard talking with Mr. Shrubs.

"Can you tell me where the mens room is?"

"Well, sir, we didn't move it."

The kid turned red. "Ha, ha, I forgot where I was for a minute."

Attendance by upperclassmen the Monday following prom is usually light. There are teachers who try to encourage the rabble to show up by scheduling tests or project deadlines for that day. The realists plan something light for the enjoyment of those who missed the gala. In Jan's classes, this activity earned extra credit, really, just for showing up. Only a few, including John and Sam, attended creative writing that day.

"Well, class, what shall we do today? We can read, write, or talk."

"How about some time to check out Instagram? Everybody that went to prom probably has their pics posted by now." The suggestion came from Sam.

Ms Miller shrugged. Social media was not in the lesson plan, but she guessed learning would be back to normal tomorrow.

Laptops and phones came out. Somebody needed the outlet to charge.

"I don't care what anybody said last week. Shrubs pulled off a really awesome prom. You couldn't even tell they were in the high school. Now I'm sorry I didn't go."

"Did you see the searchlights that night? I never saw those before anywhere, but my dad said they used to use those to draw crowds to special grand openings. And the red carpet? Like for the Oscars?"

"Whoa. Did you know Linda and Daric were going together?"

"What? Really? Let me see that."

The post showed several pics of their classmates. Arriving, all smiles. Posing next to a waterfall. Then dancing close, smiles only for each other.

"Okay, class. That's enough Instagram for today. Let's do a journal entry. Do you want me to give you a prompt, or are you good on your own?"

The photo of Linda and Daric captured a moment of intimacy. She was squeamish about invading their privacy.

John began tapping at his keyboard. He needed no prompt to vent his resentment of that smug black kid's superior attitude.

Jan opened the journal folders when she got home that afternoon. She had learned about her writing students through this ongoing assignment. Their interests, their ambitions, their worries. What she had learned about Sam was bitter. For the first few weeks it was the adolescent rage of emo rockers, but they were of a different decade. The latest entry revealed a secret that had bred and raised the rage. Stunned and embarrassed, the teacher who prided herself on knowing the kids had judged this book by its cover which dressed and moved like a sullen boy. One nobody would mess with. From her shorn head down to the Doc Martens, she looked like a ruffian.

She read on.

Another presumption proved true but underestimated. She had guessed this student's home life was unhappy, perhaps abusive. A frequent target of the rage she called Mother Superior, a judgmental parent who could never be pleased. More, Mother Superior had failed to protect her daughter from sexual assault by her father, which had been going on for quite a while. This was new and tragic information.

Holiday Weekend

The Memorial Day weekend offered Friday and Monday off from school. Most families planned for the weekend getaway, heading north to open their cottages and launch their boats for the season. Not all families left town. Teenagers were often left to amuse themselves, some with video games, others with books while their parents worked. Some seemed to sleep the entire weekend.

Sam was grateful both her parents worked at times like those. It was a relief to have the place to herself. She stretched out on the couch with The Once and Future King. For one who loved to read, it was peculiar that she had not enrolled in the challenging literature classes offered at school. She wandered into those classrooms when the door might be left open to peruse the shelves. The volume she was enjoying now was not the only in her collection with a number on the cover. She pocketed those that looked interesting from the classroom collections or from the library. She found no shame in this theft. She didn't do drugs. She did books.

Reading was her best escape from the tension in the household. Her mother berated her as lazy if she was caught doing nothing. Her father avoided pestering her if it looked like she was doing school work. And that was why she had become such an avid reader.

Sam worked at mastering the trick of predator avoidance. When she was very young, her father stroked her hair and arms and back. When she was older, he began restraining her with one arm while the other fondled and pinched. When she cried in pain, he insisted she was not hurt because he would never hurt his Sammy girl. The sexual assault progressed until now she did what she could to avoid being in a room with him.

From the couch she heard the garage door opener. It was early afternoon. No one was expected home for hours. Heavy footsteps approached the door.

"Whatcha doin', Sammy girl? Reading again? You have all weekend for that. Come over here and give your dad some sugar."

She felt her stomach lurch. That phrase meant he wanted to use her mouth.

"Aw, Dad. I am really not feeling so good today. I think I need to throw up."

That part was certainly true.

"Oh yeah? You do? Well, I got something that will take your mind off your misery." He reached for her arm, but she squirmed away and fled to her room.

She had thought about this before, something she could do to keep him away. Something at least to slow him down. She had rearranged her bedroom furniture so that a dresser was closer to the door, and now she threw her weight against it, inching it toward the door to block it.

"Don't run from me, Sammy girl. Nobody loves you like your daddy."

He threw a shoulder at the closed door, crashing it open less than an inch. The dresser held.

"It's okay, Sammy girl. I got nothing to do today. I'll wait." His voice was low. He did not sound angry. Sam vomited all over the carpet.

She had her phone and her backpack. She mopped up the sick mess with a couple dirty tee shirts. She knew she should call someone. Who? Mom? That was a laugh. Mother Superior had never been any help, and she surely knew what had been going on for years inside her home. 911? That would bring police with lights and sirens, and the neighbors would all step outside and wonder what in the world was going on at the Carlsons. And then Mom would find out, and Mom would kill her. She had absolutely no doubt. Kill her.

On the other side of the door, her father pulled a twelve-pack out of the fridge and settled in to pass the rest of the day. He pushed back in the recliner so he could keep an eye on his daughter's bedroom door. The first three beers went down fast.

Then she heard no more from him. Surely she would have heard if he had left. So he was still in the house. She dragged the dresser back from the door just enough to peek out through a crack. She saw him sprawled in his recliner, the dozen empties littering the floor. Looked like he might have been asleep. She could wait, but not for too long. She did not want her mother to come home from work and find this scene. She needed to get out of there. If only she could get quietly past the sleeping man without waking him.

She grabbed the backpack and put the phone in her jeans pocket. Opened the bedroom door just enough to squeeze through, and crept down the hall. Not the garage. Too noisy. Out the back, to the deck, out the gate. That would work. But on the way she stopped in her parents' bedroom and took a quick look around. Sometimes he kept a loaded pistol in the nightstand. It was there. She stashed it into the backpack and made her escape. She had never shot it, but if that monster came after her again, she could learn pretty quick.

The house was about a mile outside of town and the spring afternoon was balmy. She crammed her hands into her hoodie pockets, and headed toward town. She had not gone far when a familiar truck approached, headed toward her house. Her best friend Debbie was on her way to get Sam and go looking for something to do. Maybe swing by the bowling alley where Mike would be working. Maybe check out a party after that. She honked, pulled a u-turn and leaned over to open the door for her most frequent partner in crime.

"Get in here, bitch."

"Hey, bitch. Good to see you, too."

"What? Are you bringing homework with you? Don't you know we have a long weekend?"

"Yep. Three more days. Hey, Deb, do you think I could crash at your place for a while? The 'rents are more than I can stand right now."

It's not so unusual. Sometimes parents and their teenage kids just annoy each other like crazy and everybody needs a break. Happens all the time.

Ending it

Debbie and Mike had been having a fight. Again. Sam was almost used to hearing the two of them go at it. They had picked up Mike when he got off work and headed to a party at somebody's house they barely knew. There was beer and pot and loud music and sarcasm, everything necessary for a good time. Sam and Deb were both sullen and angry. They left the party to walk down the road. Mike watched them leave through the garage, shrugged, and looked around for somebody else to show off for.

"What a roaring asshole." That from Sam with a loud snort.

"I know! He really is such a roaring, fucking asshole. I don't know why I keep taking him back. I tell you he has changed. He used to be such a sweetheart."

Mike was a guy who hit women. He often left bruises on his girlfriend.

Sam stopped in the middle of the road.

"Who are you talking about?"

"Mike! How many roaring, fucking assholes do we know?"

"At least two," Sam said. "I am talking about a completely different roaring, fucking asshole. I am talking about Gerald P. Carlson, my very own daddy dearest."

When they returned to the party a few minutes later, they spotted Mike making out with another girl over in a corner.

"I'm so out of here," said Debbie.

They took Debbie's truck, leaving Mike to find his own way home, which probably wouldn't be very hard for him.

That week's journal confided the extent of her father's sexual abuse and about taking the firearm from his nightstand, which she intended to use if he tried to touch her again. She could not go home.

Teachers are, by law, mandatory reporters of child abuse. This student was seventeen years old. Old enough for emancipation. Did the law apply? If not, would protective services step in? Would that be best?

Jan was cautious about maintaining Sam's confidence and doing the right thing. She added a brief note to the entry. "Let's talk."

Sam was in danger.

Tuesday morning she went looking for Nick. Not in the boiler room, he was patrolling the parking lot. She had to admit the guy was subtle. Looked like he was just out there greeting students as they got off the buses, ever watchful. She fell into step next to him.

"I need your help, Nick."

He smiled. They really did not pay him enough.

"What's up?"

"How well do you know Sam Carlson? I'm worried. Is

she being bullied?"

"Are you kidding? Sam? There ain't nobody going to mess with Sam Carlson."

"That's what I used to think."

"What's changed?"

Jan paused, considering how much to reveal. Nick was absolutely trustworthy, and if anyone would know how to help a kid, it was him.

"I believe she's in danger. At home. I will be talking to her today, and it would help if I had something to suggest. Some place that would be safe. Otherwise I could call the police, but I don't want to make things worse."

Nick stopped and pulled out his cell. There's an emergency women's shelter run by the Y. They're good for 72 hours, but it would give her time to make a plan. He texted Jan the contact info.

A bell rang from inside the school.

"Thanks, buddy. I owe you big time."

"Yeah. Like I'd live long enough to collect." He gave her a grin and a knuckle bump. They were on the same side.

Later that day Sam lingered after the last bell. Teacher wanted to talk, she said.

Jan had called the shelter during her prep period. She explained the situation to the director and asked if they could accommodate a teenage girl. It was, she was told, a temporary emergency shelter, for women and their children in immediate danger of partner abuse. They were not equipped for long-term housing, but could put Sam in touch with a social worker. They would be expecting her after school.

The teacher explained the plan to Sam who turned pale at the prospect of running away. Of course she had considered it before, not going to Deb's house for a couple days, just taking off, no destination in mind. But this sounded like actually making a break for it.

"You have more options, Sam, and none of them are wonderful. We could contact the police. I'd go with you down to the station and you would file a complaint against your father. They would ask you some questions, and then they would go to your house and arrest him."

Sam looked horrified. Arrest her father? Mother Superior would be furious.

"Or I could file a report with CPA. That's the child protection agency. It's state government. I would tell them I had reason to believe you were in danger at your home. Then they would send a case worker to your house to do an inspection and interview both of your parents. If what they find supports my suspicions, they would remove you from the home and find a foster home for you to live in until you turn eighteen. Then you would be on your own. If the caseworker finds evidence of physical or sexual abuse, she would bring in the police who could make an arrest and file criminal charges."

Sam looked like she might vomit. How could anybody call these options? They were all so awful.

"Of course if your parents convince the case worker that everything is fine, you will get to stay at home with parents who are angry that you shared an ugly secret."

Sam felt like she might faint.

"The third choice is I can drive you over to the women's shelter right now. You can stay there for 72 hours. You will meet with a social worker and have a hearing in front of a judge who will find you safe temporary housing. You will be graduating in just a few weeks. You have a whole future to think about beyond the next 72 hours."

"Could I stop by the house to grab some things?"

"Isn't that kind of risky? Who is home right now?"

"Nobody until 6. They both work."

"Okay, then. Let's go."

The two headed out toward the faculty parking lot. Nick saw them leave and followed. He waved. They climbed into the Honda and Nick trotted up and climbed in the back seat.

"If you're going to get busted for kidnapping, I figure you'll want a witness."

He always knew just the right thing to say. Jan was glad to have him along on this errand.

Their first stop was at Sam's house. Jan pulled the car to a stop at the curb and Sam ran inside, emerging a few minutes later with a heavy looking duffle which she stashed into the back of the car with a loud thump.

"Lordy, girl, what are you packing in that thing?"

She did not answer.

The shelter was in an old farmhouse on the edge of town. No sign identified it. A privacy fence enclosed a large back yard. A wrap around porch with rocking chairs invited them to the front door, where they were greeted by a middle aged woman with a kind smile.

"Hello, Samantha," she said. "I'm Doris. You will be safe here. I need to tell you about our rules and then I will show you your room. Our guests here have been traumatized, and it is important that they feel completely safe during their stay. You will have your own room with a lock on the door. Since it is an old house, the bathroom is shared by several people who keep it tidy after they use it and don't monopolize it. There will be no drinking or illegal drugs used here. If you smoke, it must be outside. You may sit on the porch, but the backyard is kept safe and smoke-free for the children. I understand you are still in high school. The bus goes by here at 7:20, and I will let them know the driver should plan to pick you up tomorrow morning. Do you think you would like to stay here for now?

Sam was not used to having a choice about anything. "Yes, ma'am. Thank you."

"Do you expect someone might come looking for you?"

She really didn't know. There was no way they knew about this house. They probably would not be coming here. She shook her head.

"Then let's get your things moved into your room."

Sam looked at Jan and Nick. "Thank you so much."

Jan hugged her. Then she hoisted the duffel and turned to Nick.

"It's books."

She followed Doris up the stairs. She had homework to do.

Keeping young people safe from gun violence, especially in school, had vexed parents and politicians since Columbine. Everyone had a suggestion to solve the problem and none of the suggestions came with guarantees. Debates about more guns or fewer guns. Passing laws that would be difficult to enforce. 'Hardening' the buildings and installing cameras were quick easy fixes which gave parents a false sense of security, but at least the schools were doing something. Many schools had responded to the growing threat of school shootings by limiting access to the building during the school day. Secondary entrances were locked, and visitors entered through a metal detector into an area manned by security. They sign in, explain their business, and are issued a sticker identifying them as "visitor".

Nick mans this station much of the time, but a resource officer shares the duty.

Shortly after lunch a couple days later, a stranger appeared at the front entrance of the school. He wore a suit and tie and looked like a visiting administrator. Nick had not been informed to expect such a visitor, so he looked expectantly at the gentleman.

"I'm here to pick up my daughter."

Nick blocked the man's way.

"Well, sir, you should sign in right here in my logbook, and we'll see about your daughter." Nick's voice was firm.

The man passed through the metal detector and a discreet light blinked on the monitor.

The father signed the book and Nick recognized the name. This guy would not be taking any student out of there if Nick had anything to say about it. The state trooper had been meeting with the principal about implementing further security measures in the building. Jackson and his German Shepherd came around the corner. Charge moved in close and sat. Concealed carry.

Nick pulled up Sam Carlson's schedule on his iPad and headed off down the hall to locate her. Returning from his lunch break, the resource officer stepped in to cover the security desk.

Without further conversation, Nick and the trooper had established that the girl would not be leaving with this man against her will. The police officer distracted the father, without threatening arrest, while Nick checked on his daughter who was in history class fourth hour. She had not been reported absent.

He stopped outside Mike Bagley's door and interrupted the lesson as discreetly as possible. Mr. Bagley looked up.

"Excuse me. May I speak with Sam for just a moment? I'll be quick."

Mr. Bagley nodded and gestured to the girl to go to the door.

She stepped out and closed the door behind her.

"Hi Sam. Sorry about the interruption. A man who says he is your father is here to pick you up. You don't have to go with him. We can keep you safe here."

The girl's face went pale and she began to tremble. "Was he carrying?"

"Yes, he was. Set off the metal detector and all."

"That's him. What a jackass. Please don't let him see me. I never want to see him again."

"If he has hurt you, we can have him arrested and lock him up. Trooper Jackson is with him right now."

Sam looked terrified and angry and undecided what to do. She hesitated. This was no place for this conversation. Nick gestured down the hall. "Let's find a better place to talk, a quiet spot where you can breathe and think. Don't worry about Mr. Bagley. I'll let him know you didn't skip."

He sent a quick text to Jackson. Carlson would not be a problem for a while, at least. He and Sam walked briskly toward the counselors office. He wanted to get her out of sight before the bell rang for class exchange. No need to give the kids something else to gossip about.

"Who do you want me to get for you? Ms. Miller? She has her prep hour coming up."

"Yes, please. She knows what he did." Nick handed her a box of tissues. Her father had never before come to her school.

Anyone watching from a front window would have seen Trooper Jackson converse quietly with a neatly dressed middle aged man. After a few minutes, Jackson disarmed the man, handcuffed him and put him into the backseat of the Chevy Tahoe with Canine Unit on the side. He nodded to Charge who jumped into the backseat, too, to keep an eye on his perp.

Honor

After dropping some things off in their lockers, the seniors headed for the south exit at about the same time. They crossed the parking lot along with dozens of others. Some got into cars and joined the traffic line up. The rest headed down the sidewalk toward downtown, walking alone or in pairs or small groups. These afternoons were numbered for them. All were both anxious and nostalgic, in turns or simultaneously. Halfway past the softball field Daric and John fell into step together. Side eyed looks. Daric broke first. "Did I do something to you?"

John guffawed.

"I mean, I'm sorry if I did. Was it about Linda?"

John lacked the words to explain that this new guy just had so much confidence and he didn't even know it, and John was faking it for all he was worth. How does a guy express something like that? If they were younger, he might have tossed a football and that would be the end of it.

Daric had planned to turn left at the corner, as he usually did, but when they got there, John suggested something else.

"Want to see something kind of cool?"

"Sure. What'cha got?"

"Come on over to the gun range with me. I shoot there for about half an hour on Thursdays."

The two rivals turned to the right.

Daric knew that John was interested in guns. Maybe way more than interested. And that John didn't like him. He did not feel threatened, however, by this invitation, rather more like he had been offered a truce. He would see where this went.

At the range, John slipped the keycard into the lock and they entered. A curious white man stood behind a counter, greeted John, and waited to be introduced to his companion.

"Chuck, this is Daric. We are both taking that writing class I told you about. I thought maybe he could see what the range is like, if it's okay with you."

The two shook hands.

"Hello, Daric. So John has told you about my range here, has he? Did he tell you what a pain in the ass I am about my rules?

"Actually he hasn't told me much at all, except what he read in class about run 'n' shoot. He just said it was a really cool place and invited me along today."

"He wrote a story about that, did he?" Chuck chuckled. "Well, it's a members only range, but you are a visitor so you can watch from the break room. John, show your friend where the cold drinks are. Do you need any ammo today, or are you set?"

"I'm good for this time. C'mon, Daric. I'll show you around." John dropped his range bag on a bench and crossed the hall into the break room. He opened a fridge and offered to spring for a couple cold Dews. He put two dollar bills on a stack with some others and explained. "Chuck keeps the fridge filled with all kinds of cold drinks and water. No beer, because alcohol is not allowed in here. I know, I thought it was strange at first, but it's one of his rules that he's really strict about. Says drinks and guns are a bad combination. I'm pretty sure he's right." We can drink these here, but not in the range itself. Another rule. He gets all pissy about spills and mess. But the guy really knows his stuff about guns and training, so he can be as picky as he wants about his place."

Daric opened the cold drink and took a swig. He was glad John had asked him to come along today. It really was pretty cool.

"So where do you do the shooting?"

"We can leave the drinks here and I'll show you."

A few steps away was another door into the range: five numbered lanes with benches, each with a paper target hung at a distance of fifty feet.

"When we walk around in here, our guns must be unloaded. We only load them at the bench in our lane, and keep them pointed down range. This is what he calls range etiquette. It's so nobody gets shot by accident."

John clearly respected the owner Chuck. He was not showing off for Daric, but simply sharing what he had learned.

"Well, I'll get my drink and just sit outside the window here so I can watch you shoot."

"Right!"

Daric did not know very much about guns. He could tell, though, that John had been well trained when after about ten minutes the chest on the paper target silhouette was a ragged hole. He grinned at his new friend when

102

John exited, with the range bag tucked under his arm.

"That was really amazing. How long did it take you to learn to shoot like that?"

That was John's cue to talk about his dad and the deer camps as a kid, and the cache of handguns he had inherited and how Chuck was like a second dad for him who taught him how to shoot those pistols. John's resentment melted away when he saw the look of respect on the other guy's face.

Senior Honors Night was held in the auditorium for the sake of air conditioning. Participation was not mandatory, and the bottom half of the class rank generally gave it a miss. The event drew the scholars and the prize winners and recognized the proud parents of the achievers. Charlotte Johnson would be recognized, so her parents and sisters attended. Mr and Mrs. Richardson had received a invitation to attend for recognition of their son Daric. Usually a student in attendance only for his senior year would not participate in such ceremonies, but his Baltimore school had forwarded his transcript and scholarship details which sparked a consultation between his counselor and the principal, and they agreed he should be included. Some of the recognition would reflect back on them, after all.

The four-year renewable full ride to NYU was larger than any other single scholarship that year.

Mr and Mrs. Johnson would be stunned to discover that Linda's prom date - that Black Man? - was the scholarly star of Honors Night.

This is The End

The marching band were first to arrive at the football stadium on the warm Sunday. The equipment truck delivered the instruments to an adjacent practice field where band parents helped with the unloading. Musicians greeted each other with complaints about the uniforms and the heat. Those not graduating would be heading to band camp in a couple months to prepare for the fall competitions and football games, but gathering in June happened for one of two reasons: commencement or the parade. Today it was Commencement.

The procession of faculty and graduates would begin at one. Teachers met in the field house to be given their college academic robes. The group made a flock of gaudy birds, chattering about their alma maters, their velvet sleeve patches and hoods designating advanced degrees and academic majors. The usual jokes about how Old Web had managed to get into, much less graduate from, Harvard. Collegiality ran rampant.

Graduates arrived with beaming parents and resentful siblings who went off to find the best spots in the bleachers while the honored ones mingled with friends, hugging, laughing, weeping, and eventually finding where they belonged, alphabetically, outside the gates until the time for their solemn procession. Graduating members of the marching band joined the other musicians on the practice field in their academic robes. Pomp and Circumstance would be the final performance of their band career.

The principal's secretary managed the clipboard, checking off names and sniffing breath. She handed each graduate a card on which she had personally typed their names. Some things never change. It was all very exciting.

Chairs for the graduates had been arranged in rows across the yard lines. A large stage had been erected in the south facing end zone with a podium with a sound system which made the technicians nervous, chairs for dignitaries and faculty in the rows behind. By noon thirty the place was filling up and the hot June sun shone over all.

The band marched in cadence to their section on the visitors side. They entertained the crowd with show tunes.

Trooper Jackson and Charge walked leisurely laps around the sidelines and then out to the parking lot, passing arriving crowds. Charge was discreet, but he was clearly on duty.

Jackson and Charge passed Nick O'Reilly in the parking lot. Nick's job that afternoon was to just hang out there, eyes open for the inevitable handful of students whose credits came up short, who would not be walking today with their classmates. Predicting how they would handle this disappointment was a gift unique to Nick, but attention-seeking disruption was to be expected. Graduates stepped out of their way to high-five Nick.

John, Joe, and Marian arrived together. Joe made a point of introducing his lunch buddy Nick to Marian.

"This is Nick," he said. "He's my best friend at school, next to John. And this is Mom Marian. That's what I call her." He was flustered and embarrassed, realizing what he owed these two. They shook hands, grinned, and then hugged.

Marian had insisted that her son at least consider continuing his education. If he wanted, he could live at home and go to the community college for a year or two. He knew better than to argue this point. That was settled.

John was surprised to see Chuck come through the gate. He smiled and waved.

"Mom, this is my friend Chuck from the range."

"Pleased to meet you, ma'am. I was friends with your husband Marcus, too. Now there was a good man."

Marian smiled and blushed. John was not sure, but he thought he saw Chuck checking out his mom.

Even after Gloria's return, Joe had remained at Marian's house. Gloria was outraged for a bit, but she was actually relieved to be free of the burden of parenthood, and she gave Marian some money for expenses.

The Richardsons were there as well, proud and smiling. Daric had changed his mind, postponing the return east a few weeks. They approached the entrance just as the Johnsons did. Linda's parents looked embarrassed; Daric's parents were gracious. No point spoiling a celebration. The fathers shook hands, the mothers beamed, and the graduates excused themselves to go find their places in line.

Sam had spent the night before at Debbie's house and drove to the field with her friend's family. She would celebrate her moment with her friends. She did not see her parents in the crowd, but they were there, nonetheless proud of their daughter's achievement. Mr. Carlson's case would come to court in the next few weeks; meantime, the prosecutor had strongly urged him to stay away from his daughter.

Principal White had not wanted to draw attention to security concerns, but considering the news these days, he was uncomfortable about having so many people he did not know at this community event. Graduates had been given tickets to ensure seats for their families, and the majority of these people knew Ernie White and greeted him by name.

"Good afternoon, Mr. White. Bet you're glad to be getting rid of this crop, eh? I just wanna say, you always did right by my boy, and me and the missus appreciate all you've done. But he's our last, and I admit I am glad this is my last school event."

"I hear ya," thought Ernie White, "Me too. Believe me."

It's true, with all the pressure of the final few months, that every principal is relieved to wrap things up. Senioritis is a real thing, and once they know graduation is in the bag, many of those students let their lazy out. Some forget the inhibitions of decent behavior. And some just burst into tears for no visible reason. The last thing he wanted was for his school to make the news. Charge seemed satisfied. White relaxed, and headed toward the field house to put on his own robe. The crowd was left in the hands of one demanding and competent secretary and one majestic German Shepherd Dog.

Finally the first notes of Pomp and Circumstance brought the crowd to their feet and the procession began, to be posted on YouTube before dinner.

It took a few runs through the famous processional to get everybody to their seats. When it was finally managed the crowd thundered applause and the secretary bowed discreetly and stepped into the shade, her most important duty of the month accomplished. Introduction of dignitaries. It was time for the speeches. Time for elderly relatives in wheelchairs to nod off and for toddlers to squirm. Mercifully the sound system functioned without crackling static. The Valedictorian's speech was heartfelt. And then it was time to present the graduates, class officers first, then their classmates in alpha order.

And no one was shot that day.